Fatal
Twist

Jenna Skand

PublishAmerica
Baltimore

© 2003 by Jenna Skand.

First printing

ISBN: 1-59129-791-5
PUBLISHED BY
PUBLISHAMERICA BOOK PUBLISHERS
www.publishamerica.com
Baltimore

Printed in the United States of America

Dedications:

For Grandpa and Grandma, for George (Dad), and for Joyce, you all are sorely missed and thought of often.

CHAPTER ONE

Cassidy watched from the table as Julian packed his suitcase. The last three weeks had been the best in her life. Now he was leaving. Back to work, and back to being serious. No more carefree days, and passionate nights. No more long walks on the beach, or dancing 'til dawn. There would be no more hours of gentle lovemaking. She would miss him. Cassidy snapped out of her daze and looked up into Julian's handsome face. He smiled, even though she could tell that he didn't want to leave. She rested her head in his embrace as he stood in front of her. "Don't go. Stay a little while longer, Jule. Please?" she asked.

The celebrity race was in one week. If he and his partner, Mason, won, they were going to donate to their favorite charity. Mason Manis, was Julian's partner and best friend. They had grown up together in a small town, just over the Golden Gate Bridge, called San Jose. Mason's foster father was a nightclub saxophonist, and Julian's father was an architect from England. They had been friends ever since middle school.

"I can't, sweetheart. I have to go back to London and get the car ready for the race. I've already put it off a week, and there's so much to do. Besides, Mason will be meeting me in an hour or so, I can't just leave him hanging again. It would not be right," he explained for the third time.

"I know," Cassidy sat up and sighed. "How long will it be before I'll get to see you again?"

"It'll be a while, I can tell you that for sure. It's hard for me to say that to you, Cass, but it's true. I wouldn't lie to you. I want to be with you so much. Why don't you come with me?" Julian asked.

She looked down. "I can't."

"Why? You still haven't given me a good reason."

How could she answer? She thought, while making sure he had packed everything. Two months ago, when she met him, her intentions weren't to fall in love. But, only to get him in her arms long enough to break up the band he and Mason had. Suddenly, things changed, and the decision to ruin her long lost brother's life backfired.

Cassidy closed her eyes tightly, trying to shake the memory away. Julian put his arms around her waist and kissed the back of her neck. She smiled and turned to him. He had grown even more handsome since she'd met him. His chestnut hair met his shoulders, and curled slightly. His bangs were lightly streaked with blond that highlighted his deep brown eyes. She kissed him long and thoroughly.

"I'm going to miss you," he said calmly. "At least come with me to lunch. It will give us a little more time."

"I think I can manage that," she smiled. "I'll get my purse."

The patio was set, looking over the Santa Monica beach. The tables had giant umbrellas topping them. Cassidy's waist long, amber hair blew back softly. Julian lit a cigarette after ordering a light lunch and two glasses of iced tea. He leaned back watching his lover. She infatuated him. She took his breath away while he gazed at her through his rising smoke.

Her skin was just lightly kissed with the sun. Her eyes so blue they could match the most stunning sapphire in existence, actually they would put it to shame. Cassidy had this mysterious glow about her that excited him with an ultimate desire.

"What?" she asked, catching his dreamy gaze.

"Nothing," he replied, as the waitress set down their drinks.

"Tell me," Cassidy said afterward, leaning forward.

"It's just that you take my breath away. You are the most beautiful creature I've ever seen," he admitted, kissing her hand.

"Stop it. You're teasing me," she blushed.

"I've never been more serious in my life."

"Drink your tea," Cassidy laughed and waived him off, flattered.

Julian leaned back again, satisfied with her reaction to his dupe. He sipped from his glass and seeing his way through the other tables of people, he waived to his friend that was looking for him. Seeing Mason's face reminded him that their three week unplanned vacation was coming to an end. It was time for work again. Cassidy sat perfectly still, staring blankly out into the ocean as if no one was around her. But, then she noticed Julian waving to someone and she turned carefully.

Her face flushed hotly when she saw him. Quickly she stood and slipped on her sunglasses. A confrontation now would only make things worse. She needed more time to sort things out. She wasn't ready to deal with him at that moment. Cassidy threw her purse over her shoulder.

"Where are you going?" Julian asked.

"I have to use the lady's room, love. I'll be right back," she announced quickly.

"Wait a minute and I'll introduce you to Mason."

"That's OK. I can't wait," she lied.

Julian took her arm gently. "Cassidy, sit down. I really want you to meet him. What's wrong?" he asked.

"I have to use the restroom, Jule. Is that a crime? Now let me go," Cassidy exclaimed as she pulled away.

"Julian!" Mason said, moments after Cassidy disappeared.

"Hi. How was your vacation?" Julian stood and they shook hands, as he watched Cassidy push through the crowd.

"Wonderful. And yours?"

"The same," he assured and motioned his friend to sit.

"Was that the mystery lady I've been hearing so much about?" Mason asked, as he sat down.

"Yes. I can't wait for you to meet her. I know you'll just love her," Julian smiled. They talked for a while. Julian kept looking at his watch nervously, so Mason offered him a cigarette. Julian got up from the table and found a waitress. She smiled at the young man who appeared so distraught. Her smile asked how she could help him. He politely asked if she would look for Cassidy in the ladies room. She nodded and he gave her a quick description. She came back out alone, smiling sadly and apologizing. Julian thanked her and paid his bill, puzzled. Then he went back to the table.

"What's going on?" Mason asked.

"Did you bring a car?" Julian asked as he tossed a tip on the table.

"Yeah. The limo is waiting."

"I have to go back to Cassidy's apartment," Julian stated.

"All right. Let's go," Mason agreed, nodding his head. Meanwhile, Cassidy had raced back to her apartment. Blinded by tears, she rushed in the door. Suddenly, the thirteen years of waiting for her brother to find her had come to an end. She needed more time to put aside the pain and bitter hate. Time to figure out what to tell Julian. She knew he would be hurt because she had left without saying good-bye, and she knew he would be coming, soon.

Flashes of her childhood went before her eyes, bringing scalding tears of hate and rage that ran down her cheeks and dripped off her chin. She went to her desk and pulled the key from her pocket. She opened the drawer to a thick, old scrapbook. Laying it on top of the desk she began to read the newspaper clippings it held, and gazed at the black and white photograph of her parents on the inside cover.

David and Sarah Manis were tragically killed early this morning on a charter flight coming into the airport terminal. Their two children, Mason, age 10 and Cassidy, age 5 survive them. The funeral will be held on Thursday, August 10 at the Roth Funeral Home. All friends are asked to attend.

Cassidy sobbed into her hands as she read the statement

from the courts.

> It is the court's decision that since there are no living relatives the following custodial arrangements are in the best interest of the minor children, Mason and Cassidy Manis: They are to be placed in the legal and physical custody of Jackson and Linda Sanders.

Jack and Linda had been David and Sarah's best friends. Cassidy remembered how sweet and caring Linda had been. How she had learned to love her even though she couldn't quite understand where her mommy had gone. Linda would hold Cassidy on her lap for hours, rocking and singing different tunes to her in a soft voice. It was a comforting, safe time in her young life. Then Linda was gone too. Killed by a drunk driver out joyriding. It was devastating to lose her as well.

After the death of his wife, Jack Sanders was overwhelmed by grief. He turned into a very different person. He became a disillusioned drunk, and started to beat Mason and Cassidy as if Linda's death was somehow their fault. Mason rebelled against the abuse and punishments that he didn't deserve. He began causing trouble with the boys at school. Jack decided that Mason wasn't worth all the problems he was causing and cleaned up long enough to send him off to the authorities.

Cassidy got from the desk and threw herself on the bed. She could still remember the day he had gone away. A businesslike woman stepped from a long black car, complete with an official-looking seal on the door. She came in and Jack ordered Mason to pack all his things. When he refused, Jack tugged him up the stairs. Cassidy remembered standing by his bed watching him. She had been young enough to still wear her hair in pigtails and cling to baby dolls for comfort. Her brother had knelt in front of her and straightened her ruffled blue dress.

"Cassie, I want you to be a good girl and wait until I come back for you. Will you do that for me?" Mason had always called her "Cassie," like their mother had done.

"But, where are you going?" she asked.

"I don't really know for sure. But, I will be back," he promised.

"I don't want you to go away, Mason. You won't come back. Just like Mommy and Daddy and Linda," Cassidy started to cry.

Mason hugged his little sister. "I will, Cassie. I promise you I will."

"NO!" she sobbed and clung to him.

Jack stormed back upstairs and forced Mason to go down with his suitcase. Cassidy was crying and screaming to go with her brother, kicking Jack as he held her back. Mason freed himself from the woman and ran back to hug his sister again. Then he turned to face Jack.

"I'll be back for her, Mr. Sanders. I swear I'll come back for her. You'd better not lay a hand on her or you'll pay for it. I swear!" Mason said defiantly and then he was dragged away and shoved into the car.

Julian was nervously smoking a cigarette on the way to the apartment. Mason patted his friend heartily on the shoulder. The entire situation was almost amusing to him. Truly it would have been if Julian weren't so irritated with him for smiling to himself. He tried to change the subject.

"What did you say this girl's name is, Julian?" Mason asked.

"Cassidy. Cassidy Mantis," he replied.

"Mantis?"

"Yeah. Do you know her?" Julian asked curiously.

"No. I don't think so. The only girl I ever knew with that name was my sister," he said sadly.

"What happened to your sister? I remember you telling me before, but I don't remember what you said exactly."

"I was told she died of pneumonia. I'd rather not talk about it. My sister was all I had after our parents were killed. I'll never forgive myself for deserting her the way I did." He looked away.

"From what I understand, Mason, you didn't have much of a choice," Julian pointed out. "I'll be right back," he called after getting out of the car, when it had come to a stop in front of the apartment building.

Cassidy still lay on her bed sobbing. She had mascara dripping down her cheeks, mixed with her tears. When she heard Julian's key turning in the lock, she ran into the bathroom, and slammed the door shut. She didn't know what she should say to him. Mason was her brother. With he and Julian's fame and fortune, it made it even more difficult to explain. There were people trying to scam celebrity's all the time. What would make her story any different?

Julian heard the slam as he walked down the hallway. When he came in the bathroom, she was splashing cold water on her face. She caught his reflection, in the mirror, when she looked up from the sink. She turned and her tears came again, uncontrollable. He didn't know what to say. Seeing her so upset melted him.

"Jule, I ..."

"I think I know someone you've been avoiding for a long time, Cass," he began, while drying her face. "I don't like games, especially when you knew who I was all the time." Her crying seemed almost too much for him to take when he wanted nothing more than to hold her. He had no idea what she was going through. "Have you just been using me? Were the last three weeks a charade? Do you really care for me?" his many questions were thrown at her in a confusing barrage.

"How can you ask me that? I love you more than I can say at this point, Julian. That's what this is all about. I fell in love with you, and all my plans to get back at Mason exploded in my face. And, who doesn't know who you are," Cassidy explained. She felt like she was going crazy. She was afraid of losing the only man she had ever been able to love. She moved to hug him, and he held her tightly at first, but then pulled away.

He wouldn't look at her. "Why? All I want to know is, why? What did Mason do to you that could make you want to hurt him so badly? How could you use me to get to him? I don't understand."

"He left me. He got into trouble and left me. Then he promised he would come back. I was only seven, and already I had lost my parents, and the only other woman that could comfort me. Then I lost Mason, too. My only brother. While he lived with people who cared about him, I was abused and molested; from the day he left, until the day I finally got away." She tried not to cry, but couldn't help the rage she felt welling up within her.

"What?" Julian turned.

"Mason Manis is my brother, Julian. In August 1972, he promised me that he would come back. He never came. How was I supposed to get away? I was only seven! So I waited, and waited for him to come, he never did," her voice seemed to soften, but still echoed the resentment that had built over all those years. "When I was seventeen I got a job and made something of myself, until I could find out where he was and how he ticked," she smiled. "The both of you did it for me, by becoming famous."

Julian was silent. He had just seen a side of Cassidy he didn't think was possible. It was heartbreaking to know about her childhood. Yet, she had kept her backbone and started fresh, and tried to forget what a sickened man had done to her. Suddenly, Julian felt guilty for all the fun and games he and Mason had enjoyed, while his sister was enduring such horrors. All that she had worked so hard to have, Mason was handed on a silver platter.

"I thought if I could get you to be with me, he would be furious. You haven't had a great reputation with women, Jule. All I had to do was get you to break up the band. It wasn't hard to figure out," she sat up and sighed. "It was just my luck that you are the most caring, gentle man I've ever met. I just couldn't go through with it. I couldn't hurt you, or him."

"There's just one thing you didn't know. One thing that would have changed everything for you," Julian said.

"What's that?"

"Mason thought you were dead. As long as I've known him, if he had known you weren't he would have

14

contacted you right away. He's always blamed himself for your death," Julian took a deep breath. "I think it's time you and your brother were reunited, and I don't need to be in way," he finished, and left the apartment.

Cassidy cursed herself for being so secretive. Now her revenge had gotten in the way. She couldn't lose Julian, and she darted out the door to go after him. At the top of the stairs, she saw Mason with Julian behind him. Unsure of her emotions she ran back into her apartment. She felt a wave of heat flush her face as she panicked. Then she swung around when she heard their voices in the doorway.

Mason paused while he focused on her. A long silence seemed to fill the room, and then he reached out and embraced her. There was no question that this was his sister in his arms. He moved her out to arms length, but did not let her go. She looked like their father, except for her eyes; those were very much mother's eyes. He gently touched the thick mane of amber hair, hoping to bring back the little girl he had been forced to leave behind, so many years ago. He pulled her close again, and held her tightly for a long time.

"You're even more beautiful than I imagined you'd be," he stated, the happiness he felt threatened to choke the voice from him. He could actually feel it fill his entire body, along with the realization that Cassidy was not dead.

"Mason, I don't know what to say," her voice quivered. "I ... feel ... so terribly bad for the things ... I thought you deserted me." Cassidy began to sob once again.

"I'm so sorry. It's over, Cassie. It's all over. We're together now, and that's all that matters," Mason said. "You're alive. Thank God, you're alive!"

Julian was standing by the door watching this touching moment between his best friend and the woman who had stolen his heart. Now they were brother and sister as well, there was so much pain and so much love in that very moment. More than anything there was no more blame. He had never seen Mason as happy as he was right now.

After rescheduling their flight to London, Mason and Cassidy sat to talk. Julian sat at the table with them as Mason encouraged Cassidy to come with them. The chauffeur helped them bring her three suitcases out to the waiting limousine. Julian waited on the balcony. Cassidy came out and leaned on the railing beside him. She stared off into the lights of Santa Monica, glowing in the darkness. She softly put her hand over his.

"What's on your mind, Julian?" she asked.

"I don't want to talk right now, Cassidy. I thought I knew you. I thought for one time in my life, I'd finally found a love that didn't need lies or games. I thought love was supposed to be complete, like ours appeared to be. But, you were going to use me and throw me away like nothing, Cass," he laughed slightly and sighed. "You've hurt me. That's something no woman has been able to do to me," he finished and walked away, leaving her to stare after him.

CHAPTER TWO

On the plane Cassidy sat between both men. Julian stared out the window at the darkness below. He inhaled from his cigarette deeply, trying to shut out the incessant chatter of his partner. Cassidy's musky perfume was filling his nostrils and made him weary with the want to feel her fingers in his. His gentle feelings for her overrode his aching heart. He fell asleep, dreaming of the last three weeks they had spent together.

Mason watched as his sister looked upon his friend with such loving eyes. She gently took the burning cigarette from his fingers before covering him with a blanket she had gotten from a stewardess. Then she kissed his cheek and smoothed his hair. Smiling, she turned back to look at Mason, who was watching her so curiously. When she studied him closely, she could almost remember her mother's face. And, she smiled his way.

"Do you love him, Cassie?" he asked.

"More than I can say," she replied with a nod.

"He's never been in love before. Promise me you'll be careful. I don't want to you get hurt," Mason stated.

"One thing I think you should know, Mason, is Julian has a side I bet you didn't know he had. A gentle side," Cassidy explained with pride.

"I've seen women walk in and out of his life, he never loved any of them." Mason lit up a cigarette. "Julian's like a brother to me, so don't get me wrong, but I've seen him hurt a lot of women who cared for him very much."

"He told me that. I think he has a lot of love to give, but he just hasn't found the right person to give it to, yet," Cassidy protected her lover from her brother's harsh insinuations.

Mason smiled to himself. She was no longer the frightened little girl he used to know, she had become very strong since he had seen her last. Mason would never be able to see her as anyone other than his little sister. All that mattered to him was that she was alive, and with him. Now, he could give her all the things he so wanted to, before Jack Sanders had lied to him.

They were groggy getting off the plane in London. Cassidy was jostled as Mason and Julian moved to protect her from their adoring fans. The thousands of screaming teenage girls held up banners with welcoming smiles and admiration. Mason and Julian signed countless autographs before they were ushered into their waiting limousine by security guards.

Both men sighed as they pulled away from the terminal and onto the highway. Cassidy turned to Mason as he picked up the phone to make a call. Julian leaned back into the seat and put his feet up. The interior was a basic plush gray, and it held a bar on the side. A television set played the local newscast of some kind. Cassidy stared at the unfamiliar surroundings in amazement.

"What was all that at the airport, Julian?" she asked. "How did they know you'd be there?"

"Well … it all depends. Sometimes groupies will overhear conversations at concerts, and sometimes newsletters are printed out for the fan clubs. The girls in the airport were members of one of the clubs," he replied numbly.

"Yes, but, how did they know after you rescheduled the flight?"

"That we have yet to find out," he smiled to himself while he tried to puzzle it out.

Mason laughed. "We'll see you tomorrow then, Nick. OK. Cheerio." He hung up.

"Nick?" Cassidy asked.

"Our manager, Nick Kane. Just letting him know we're back," Mason explained.

"Isn't it strange that a fan club knows you're back before your manager?" she laughed.

"We're used to it," Julian stated, and Mason nodded in agreement.

"This is definitely going to be a completely new experience," she said.

After an hour, Mason pulled Cassidy to his side so she could see the mansions for the first time. The limo stopped at a long iron gate, and waited for it to open. They drove in. Many high green bushes lined the long drive until it split into two directions. It was like watching a documentary on television. A giant fountain spilled water between the two mansions.

They drove to the right and paused in front of one. Julian got out and pulled his suitcase from the trunk. Cassidy looked his way, hoping that he would ask her to stay with him. He said nothing, simply went up the walk and disappeared into the house. Disappointed, she watched the spot where he had entered, hoping he would reappear.

Her heart ached for him, and then Mason took her hand and squeezed it.

The enormous foyer was below a balcony. A large staircase was on the left, gracefully circled upward. Off to the right was a living room with royal blue carpeting, the furniture was white, and looked very comfortable. The sofa appeared to be the type you would sink right into. Behind this was a small white piano adorned with a simple blue vase of lilies. The entire room was decorated in deep shades of blue, or crisp white.

Cassidy only glanced the other way, as she was climbing the stairs. She passed no less than six rooms with double doors before Mason opened one at the end of the right wing. He smiled and motioned for her to step through the doorway. The room she was being shown filled her with a sense of awe. Everything in it seemed to be fine enough for royalty to have stayed here. The room was primarily ivory, accented with the deepest burgundy, in lace and bows.

A maid entered the room and listened as Mason gave her some brief instructions. Soon Cassidy heard water running in a room to the left of the bed. She bit her lip pensively as she turned the corner. She stopped in amazement as her eyes fell upon the bathtub, she had seen tubs like this in movies and on soap operas. It was made of marble, the same shade of burgundy as accented the bedroom. The faucets and handles were golden, and ivory towels that looked like small blankets hung on golden rods. She began to feel like the fairy tale princess who has just been awakened by the handsome prince.

"I had this designed just for you, Cassie. It made me

feel better to do something in your honor. This room has never been used," he smiled.

"I don't know what to say, Mason. It's so beautiful ..." she struggled for words, but could find none.

"Say you'll stay long enough for us to get to know each other again."

Cassidy crossed the room and hugged him tightly. "I missed you, Mason. I'll stay."

"I love you. You don't know how good it is to know you are all right," he said, and kissed her lightly on the cheek before he left, the maid following behind him.

Gazing around the room a second time, Cassidy smiled and fumbled with her suitcase for a nightgown. She sank into the mass of bubbles, and hot perfumed water that had been left for her. But, once she was alone and relaxed, all she could think of was Julian. She washed up and wrapped herself in one of the soft towels. She then sat at the vanity and tried to choose from the selection of silver handled brushes and combs. She finally chose a comb and ran it gently through her waist long hair. When her hair gleamed like a fire she was satisfied and slipped into her nightgown.

Cassidy sat on the edge of the soft bed and smiled as she lay back. Not even a princess would feel a pea under this mattress, she thought to herself. The sweet smile, that warmed her face as she relaxed, remained as she fell into a dreamless sleep.

Later that evening, Mason came in and switched on a lamp. Cassidy sat up, rubbing her eyes. Getting used to the time difference between California and England wasn't going to be easy. She watched as Mason laid three different gowns over a chair.

"I trust you are a size six?" he asked.

"How did you know that?" she asked.

"Lucky guess," he sighed. "Julian and I have decided to take you to our favorite club. Are you up to it?"

"Julian?" Her eyes brightened.

"Yes. I understand you two are an item these days."

She looked away. "I don't believe we are anymore. I've pretty much ruined our relationship."

Mason sat down next to her and put his arms around her shoulders, pulling her to him. "Don't worry, sweetheart. I'm sure he'll snap out of it."

"I hope so. He's become so very important to me," she replied and tried to smile for him.

Julian sat at the table sipping his wine, watching Mason and Cassidy on the dance floor. This elegant Italian restaurant had a small instrumental band that was playing softly. It was very peaceful and easy to relax here tonight.

All night Mason and Cassidy had reminisced about their childhood, focusing primarily on the happy times before their parents had died. They laughed while they told Julian stories while they ate dinner. He watched them now as they danced together so happily.

Cassidy shimmered in a long gown of white that hugged her hips, and fell to her ankles, just above the matching shoes. Her amber hair was braided and wrapped around her head, resembling a crown.

He had never seen her smile so brightly or heard her laugh so freely. Julian lit yet another cigarette, and inhaled deeply, hoping the rising smoke would camouflage his gaze. When the song ended she and Mason clapped, then he escorted her back to the table.

"Will you dance with me for a while, Julian?" Cassidy asked. "I do believe I've worn Mason out."

"I suppose one dance won't hurt," he replied, crushing out his cigarette.

He stood then, and held out his hand. Cassidy smiled and took it, as he led her back to the dance floor, and held her in his arms. She gratefully rested her head on his shoulder. He closed his eyes, wanting to pull her closer, but refused. The smell of her perfume was driving him mad with the desire to kiss her, but he ignored it.

"Jule, thank you so much for making me face him. I needed him back in my life. There is so much I have missed about him, and so much for me to learn about him. If you can't forgive me, I'll try and understand. I hope no matter what we can still be friends," she stated sincerely.

"I'm not sure I can trust you to be anything more," Julian replied, coldly.

Cassidy looked up at him. His face was expressionless, even his eyes seemed to be made of stone. As hers filled with hot tears of disappointment and pain, she slowly backed away from him. She turned and stumbled toward the ladies room, trying desperately to see through the wall of tears that blinded her.

Mason stood up at their table and shot his friend a disgusted look. They waited in silence for her to return. When she finally came back all of them agreed the evening was over and they should return home.

Julian sat alone in his den cursing. He began to drink the contents of his liquor cabinet alphabetically. He was in the midst of this process when Mason entered the smoky den. Seeing the condition Julian was in, Mason could only shake his head sadly. He took his friend's now empty glass over to the desk. After searching the desk for a few minutes, he located the key for the liquor cabinet and locked it up. He then slipped the key into his own pocket.

Julian's drunken gaze fell on him, and then he was favored with a sloppy smile. Mason again shook his head in disbelief. This was not like Julian at all, to drink so much was very much out of character for him. Julian staggered around the den, finally locating his glass. Upon discovering that it was empty he shattered it in the fireplace. The flames rose briefly and then settled back down. He made his way over to the desk and struggled with his cigarette pack. Mason almost found himself laughing as he watched Julian trying first to remove a cigarette from the pack, and then to meet the end of it with a lighter. Julian then offered him one, which he accepted with a small smile.

"Where's my bottle?" Julian asked, already looking as if he were going to pass out at any moment.

"I put it away. You've had more than enough this evening. I didn't come to save you, you know. It seems you wouldn't remember it tomorrow, anyway," he sighed. "Julian, if you love her, don't hurt her."

"Now that you find out — sshe's your sssister — suddenly shee's off limits. Sooo — now I get these disgusted looks." He leaned over feeling dizzy. "If she were — my sissster, more power to her. Sshe'd have … my … my blessings. Don't you — trust me?" Julian shouted suddenly.

"Jule, I think you've seen what you wanted to see. You

are still hurt because she lied to you," Mason pointed out. Julian turned away. "Sshee was going to — use me. Hoowwouldyou feel? Tell me that big brother."

"I don't know. Probably hurt, like you," he replied.

"Oh, come on, Mason, what about — Shalane? Every time that woman — ccommes around — you end up jusslike I am right now. Sshez even put moves on me, did you know that?" Julian fell victim to a fit of hiccups.

Mason had felt very bitter and angry after learning Shalane had tried to seduce his best friend. He would have loved to wring her pretty neck when that had come to light.

Shalane Taylor, had walked into his life one day, and brought nothing but heartbreak with her. Although she was a very beautiful woman to look at, that was as far as it went. Beneath that shell was a very vulgar, promiscuous individual. Mason had fallen in love with her so he would not have to be alone.

It seemed he didn't have any kind of hold on her at all. She did what she wanted, when she wanted, and sadly with whomever she wanted. She had used him to open the doors to the glamorous life he led. He gave her everything and she took it all, then she would disappear for days, then weeks and now months. But she always came back for more. All these memories only infuriated him and he frowned. He looked at Julian quizzically, had she been here again, tonight?

"What did she want this time?" he asked.

"Money, and a little night action," Julian replied. He seemed to be sobering up just slightly. "Don't worry, Mason. I wouldn't do something like that to you. We've been friends far too long. Shalane doesn't interest me, anyway."

Mason changed the subject. "We're not talking about Shalane. We're talking about Cassie."

"I'm tired now. I have a lot of work to do starting tomorrow. I'm too tired to talk anymore tonight." Julian crushed the cigarette that had burned away in his hand and flopped across the leather sofa.

"All right, Jule. I'll grant you a reprieve, for now. Go get some sleep," he said and then left.

As Mason reached the top of the stairs in his own house, thinking only of his comfortable bed and feeling very weary, Cassie appeared in her doorway. She had been pacing back and forth when she heard him enter the house. He smiled and hugged her as they walked to the doors of his own bedroom. He opened the door and turned to look at her. He could tell that she was worried about Julian, and had been waiting for some news. He brushed her long silky hair back over her shoulders and kissed her gently on the forehead.

"Why don't you go see him, Cassie?" Mason pulled the keys to Julian's house and liquor cabinet out of his pocket and folded them into Cassie's hand. She thought for a moment, biting gently on her lower lip.

"God, she looks so much like Mother," Mason thought.

Suddenly her face lit up. "I'll do just that, Mason. Thank you." She threw her arms around his shoulders and kissed him quickly on the cheek. "Thank you very much." Then she was gone.

Julian had almost made it into bed. He appeared to be stopped in the middle of falling out. He had managed to remove his shirt, but was sleeping soundly in spite of his position and state of dress. Cassidy gently rolled him completely onto the bed and began to undress him the rest of the way. She then pulled the blankets up around him, and kissed him on the cheek. Julian opened his eyes ever so slightly and stared at her groggily. He half smiled as he realized that she was really there.

"Go back to sleep. I'll stay with you," she promised.

"Are you sure? I've acted like a fool," he frowned.

"I'm in love with a fool then," she smiled.

Julian hugged her. "This fool loves you more than anything. I'm sorry, Cass." He fell asleep, as she cradled his head and brushed the hair from his eyes.

She slipped down beside him and wrapped herself in his arms. Welcoming the familiar scent of his cologne, and the warmth of his embrace, she, too, drifted off to sleep.

CHAPTER THREE

The Birmingham Auto Track was set for the race that was to be held that afternoon. In less than an hour the noise would be deafening. Julian was talking with his mechanics and Mason. Cassidy stood in the pit holding his gloves and helmet. She gazed around at the fans, drivers, and cars that were getting last minute check-ups. She wasn't sure of what would happen today. She'd never seen a race let alone actually been to one. She was nervous and unsure, and frightened by the obviously dangerous aspects of what was going on around her.

Julian stood calmly by his car, dressed in a white asbestos suit with blue stripes down the sleeves. He and the mechanics were checking his car as she stepped off to the side and stared at the large crowd of people gathering in the stands. Some were buying souvenirs, and some were purchasing snacks from the various venders that were wandering the stands. She tried to focus on the activity in the stands, rather than the impending race. She feared the butterflies in her stomach would be all too apparent to Julian, if she didn't get them under control.

He looked over at her as her hair gently blew back in the soft breeze. It seemed to be a clear day, which was unusual for this time of the year, particularly in this part of England. He had expected it to be a bit dreary and not so bright. He gazed back at Cassie, this time she caught his stare. Though she smiled at him, it was not the steady smile she usually favored him with. How could he have ever doubted her love for him? He thought he felt her tremble as they embraced. He was glad they were able to clear the air between them before the race. It kept him calm and allowed him to focus on what he must do today. All the bad feelings were gone, and the race was the next step in their lives. He held her tight.

"All of this really scares me, Jule. I don't understand it." She tried to smooth down his wind blown hair.

"I've driven a million times, Cass, and sometimes it still scares me, too," Julian agreed. "But, my mechanics are the best and my car is in perfect shape, so it's up to me, now."

"I can't help it. I've never seen you race before. I feel much better in a crowd of screaming teenage girls," she smiled crookedly.

"Me too," he laughed.

"Very funny, Julian Drake." Cassidy slapped his arm teasingly.

"Funny," echoed Mason, as spectators were cleared from the track and the drivers were instructed to get into their cars. Cassidy and Mason left the pit area to watch the race.

Julian got into his car and drove to the starting line. All the motors revved and the crowd waited impatiently. The pace car led the drivers around the track as they warmed their tires and fell into their assigned positions. Julian was fourth in a line of twenty cars. When the pace car pulled away from the pack, the green flag dropped.

Julian pulled from the front of the pack, glad the less experienced drivers were behind him. Soon he was with the faster qualifying drivers.

The announcer was shouting: "Watch J.D. in car fourteen. He's used every opportunity to pass and now he's — Wait, the yellow flag, a car has hit the wall in turn three." The drivers automatically slowed, in response to the yellow flag, and stayed to the inside of the track while emergency crews cleared the debris from the track.

"Mason, why haven't any of the drivers come into the pits?" Cassidy asked. "Don't they have to get gas yet?"

"They've only completed eight laps," Mason explained. "Now they will line up single file instead of by two's, and Julian will be in fourth place. He's doing great! Look. The green flag is coming out. Watch him move!"

Everything was a multi-colored blur to Cassidy as the cars flew around the track. The eight place cars seemed so evenly matched, and then Julian slipped past two cars on the inside of the back straightway.

The crowd was cheering for him as the announcer said: "J.D. in car fourteen is now in sixth place and thirty laps have been completed. Watch the first turn! A car is sliding sideways in front of the pack! The leaders are scattering to avoid colliding with the out-of-control car. The yellow flag is out again, for the second time in thirty laps."

"Come on, Julian, pass another car!" yelled Cassidy. "You can do it. This is so exciting!" She turned to Mason.

"Cassie, you can't pass under the flag," explained Mason. "And it's still too soon for the drivers to pit for any reason. Well … unless they feel like something is wrong with their car. Usually, they can go about fifty laps before they need tires and gas. Relax."

"Right, relax," muttered Cassidy. "That's my heart out

there. Things are happening so fast and you're telling me to relax? They are going a hundred and ninety miles an hour."

"Cassie, did you look inside the car? There are roll bars you can't see, under the hood and trunk area, and everything is reinforced around the driver's seat," Mason patiently told her while keeping an eye on the track. "Julian is safer on the track than he is on the highway. Believe me, his crew is excellent."

"But, already two cars have crashed," cried Cassidy.

"Yes, but, no one was hurt," Mason said. "Those cars are very safe and the drivers are experienced, so just try to relax and enjoy the race. Watch Julian."

"Is he still in sixth place?" Cassidy asked, as they heard that the field was clear and the drivers were once again under a green flag.

"As the speed increases going into turn one, J.D. is in sixth place and looking for an opportunity to pass," said the announcer, almost as if he had heard Cassidy's question. She smiled.

Twenty more laps went by in a flash of speed and excitement. Julian was now in third place and many of the cars that had started in the rear of the pack had now dropped out. The three lead driver's had lapped around four more times. It was difficult for Cassidy to keep track of Julian's place. She hated to interrupt her brother's concentration with so many questions, so she held her breath and watched.

"Julian! Look out!" she screamed as the lead car flew by them, going into the third turn. "There's another crash! Stop the race!"

The lead car couldn't get around the tangle of cars in the middle of the track and hit them at full speed. Fenders and other pieces of twisted metal flew through the air as cars continued to spin out of control. One of them hit the wall and flipped onto its top, then slid into the infield. Flames poured from the lead car as it slammed into the wall. The driver rolled out of his window and ran away just as it exploded in a great fireball. Everything was going in slow motion as Cassidy stood in shock. The drivers were trying to get around the cars in the middle of the track. Too much was happening all at once. Cassidy could not see Julian's car, anywhere.

"Where is he, Mason?" she cried in alarm.

"He's OK, now let go. You're choking me," Mason yelled. "He and the second place car made it past the crash site. See their tracks in the infield? They're OK. Look … open your eyes and look, Cassie."

"I think I'm going to be sick," she moaned. "Why don't they stop the race? Why are they still out there?"

"Cassidy, haven't you ever been to a race before? Watch what's happening. These are professional drivers. They will finish the race. As soon as they can move again under the yellow flag. The race will continue. All those laps count. Hasn't Julian told you anything about racing? He should have taken you to see at least one. Wait until I have a chance to talk to him."

"He's really OK? And the rest of the drivers are OK, too?" She peeked out from behind his shoulder, as the announcer echoed her thoughts.

"The drivers are out of their cars and no one appears to be injured. Let's race! The green flag is out again with only ten laps to go. Ladies and gentlemen, J.D. is in second place and he has his work cut out for him. The driver of car sixty-nine has more experience behind the wheel."

"Only ten laps to go? Wonderful." Cassidy breathed. "Only ten laps," she smiled.

Julian was on the lead car's tail as they flew around the track. It seemed as though they were the only two cars moving. Time and time again he tried to pass, only to drop back as they came into a turn.

"Cassie, he can pass him. His car is faster," said Mason carefully. "Look he pulls even with him in the straightway."

"Isn't second good enough?" cried Cassidy. "Only two more laps left."

"Not for Julian," explained Mason. "Watch him push the leader. He's hoping to push him into a turn too fast, and look the white flag is out. One lap to go."

"Mason, it's happening just like you said," Cassidy screamed.

The crowd rose to its feet behind them, cheering wildly. "JULIAN ... JULIAN ... JULIAN!" Cassidy found herself drawn in and chanting with them.

Suddenly he shot around the lead car into first place, just in time to take the checkered flag. The noise of the crowd was deafening. Julian held the checkered flag high as he circled the track alone.

"It's the 'Victory Lap,' Cassidy," Mason explained. "Now we can go down and see him. He won!"

"I'm just glad it's over," she smiled and sighed.

They pushed through the crowd of people milling

around the cars that were stopped on the track. Everyone was trying to congratulate Julian at the same time. Hundreds of adoring fans surrounded him as he tried to get out of his car. He held up his flag and the crowd began to cheer again. He slipped off his helmet and searched the crowd until his eyes met Cassidy's eyes. Then no one else seemed to exist except for her. After he was given his trophy and had his picture taken with Mason and Cassidy, they slipped away.

He put his hands on her face, and her hands covered his. He smiled into her eyes. "Were you scared?" he asked.

"Terrified," she smiled. "I'm so happy for you. You were great out there, and then I knew I was the luckiest woman in the world to have your love."

"No. I'm the one that's lucky to have you," he said and kissed her deeply. Then he caught her up in a happy embrace and swung her around.

Mason watched from a distance, wondering how long it would last for Julian. How long would he love Cassidy before he became bored with her? Julian had never actually been in love; it had always been infatuation. This made Mason worry about what his sister might have to go through. Still, they seemed so happy, and Julian looked at her in a way that Mason had never seen before.

"Let's go home," Julian said and put his hand around hers. "I'd like you to stay with me, in my home from now on. If you're willing?"

"There's nothing more I could ask for," she said, as he opened the car door for her. After she was seated he closed it firmly.

Later that night Julian and Cassidy arrived at Mason's

house. As they entered the darkened house, the lights suddenly flashed on as all of Mason and Julian's friends jumped out to congratulate him on his victory. They carried the trophy to its place of honor, in the middle of the buffet table, and Mason raised his glass to make a toast.

"To my partner and the number one race car driver in all of England!" Everyone agreed and joined him in a champagne toast.

The buffet was full of wonderful finger-foods and all were having a wonderful time. Cassidy sipped at her champagne, looking around at all the people crowding in on Julian. She wanted him to herself more than anything at that moment. She noticed that a beautiful red head had gotten Mason's attention, and smiled to herself. It soon became apparent that the two of them were arguing and she began to move protectively toward her brother.

At that moment Julian caught her gently by the arm. "Don't, Cass, I don't want you to see what that woman does to him," he warned.

"Who is she?" inquired Cassidy, clearly upset.

"Shalane Taylor. Don't worry about it. She'll be gone soon. He hasn't heard from her in months, so it is very likely she only wants money. She has gotten very used to his lifestyle, as long as it doesn't directly involve him."

"What!" whispered Cassidy loudly. "I'm not going to let some money hungry tramp manipulate my brother."

Julian took a moment to ask a friend to find Cassidy something a bit stronger than the champagne that was in her trembling hand. He then turned back to her with a resigned look on his face. "Cassidy, it is out of our hands.

Believe me, I've tried to reason with him. He is blind to all but her charm."

Cassidy would hear nothing of it. She pulled away from him and darted between two people and straight to Mason. Shalane stood back and fell silent as Cassidy made eyes at Mason and led him away to dance. Shalane gave them a disgusted look and stormed out of the room. They watched her exit, both of them hoping she was leaving for the rest of the night. Mason hugged Cassidy, and seemed to relax.

"Who is that woman?" Cassidy asked, though she was pretty sure she guessed.

"My girlfriend. Nothing to worry about, Cassie," he replied, much too quickly, and flashed her his patented smile.

"You are in love with her. That is obvious by the way you looked at her. Why were you fighting?" she asked, not willing to let this go that easily.

"Just a lover's spat — " He was cut off.

"May I cut in?" Julian interrupted.

"No!" Cassidy snapped, turning to Julian, her eyes softened. "I need to finish speaking with Mason."

Mason was striding toward his den when she turned back around. He obviously thought the conversation was over with. Cassidy shook her head sadly, then took the hand Julian offered her and let him lead her into the middle of the floor.

As Mason entered his den, Shalane was sitting in a chair in front of his desk. There was smoke rising from the cigarette she held, but the rage in her eyes burned even hotter. As Mason sat down at his desk she crushed out her cigarette, then delivered a brutal slap to his handsome cheek. He didn't have time to get out of the way, and could only sit there stunned as the perfect red imprint of her hand rose on his face.

"Who was she?" snarled Shalane. "My replacement? Have you been running around on me?"

"That was my sister, Shalane. I didn't get a chance to tell you before you insisted that I write you a check," he replied flatly, hoping that his desire to kiss her didn't show.

Shalane then draped herself across his lap and began to nuzzle his neck. She stroked his cheek, which was still red from the slap she had delivered with the same hand only moments before. "Have you written it yet?" she purred in his ear.

"No, you didn't give me a chance before you started your inquisition," he answered, shifting uncomfortably beneath her.

"Don't you want me?" she asked petulantly.

"Stop it, Laney. I'll write your check," he said, pushing her off his lap. She leaned over his shoulder so that the expensive perfume she wore lingered in his nostrils.

Mason unlocked the desk drawer and pulled out his checkbook. He found a pen and began to fill out a check. Shalane reached for it before he had even finished. He pushed her hand away and filled in a large amount. He hesitated before signing it. Shalane smiled and leaned over so he could see down the front of her tight red dress. She kissed his cheek, and then turned his face so she could kiss his lips. He tried to pull away from her again, but she laughed and drew him back.

"You can't turn me away, Mason. You love me. You

know you need me," she said huskily as she ran her fingers over his chest. "Do you know why I've come back so soon?"

"Why?" he whispered into her neck as he reached behind her to undo the zipper of her dress.

"I had to use the last of the money you gave me to abort the baby we made last time," she replied in a calculated tone.

The flush of desire faded as quickly as it had come over him. Shalane began to laugh at his anguish, even as tears began to flood his blue eyes, and then run down his cheeks. She quickly zipped her dress and stuffed the check into her brassiere. As she sashayed across the den she turned long enough to blow him a kiss, which hit him harder than her slap had. "Cheerio, Daddy-O!"

Cassidy came through the door a few moments later and found him with his face in his hands, his shirt still unbuttoned. She quickly went to him and instinctively put her arm around his shoulders. "Mason?" she said.

"Cassie, go away. I don't want you to see me like this," he replied, his voice quivering.

"Why? Because it's not glamorous? What don't you want me to see, that you have feelings? That you can be hurt, just like the rest of us? Remember that I've seen you at your worst. I've seen you suffer far worse than this. Tell me what she did to you, Mason?"

Mason Looked up at her then, with tears in his eyes. "She killed our child. She had an abortion, Cassie. She just did it without even telling me I could have a child. God, I can still smell her perfume on my shirt and hands. She's like a disease."

Cassidy held him while he sobbed. Neither of them noticed Julian standing silently in the doorway, he quietly turned and left before they could.

It was hours before he found her, but Shalane was predictably in a bar. Julian pulled her off the dance floor, where her partner had been holding her up with one hand inside her dress and the other on the back of her neck. Julian slapped some cash down on the bar in front of the bartender and then shoved her out the door. Shalane stood, half falling over, against the alcove just outside the door. Julian slapped her face in an effort to sober her up some and get her attention. "Give me the check Mason gave you," Julian growled.

"Why, you wanna give me a bigger one?" she giggled.

"You filthy, whore! I won't have you coming around anymore. Do you hear me? You've used Mason for the last time. I don't care what you think you have to tell the press, we will have you arrested for harassment."

"You can't do that to me," she said, beginning to sober.

"No? It won't be too hard to follow the trail of checks with your endorsement on them," Julian snapped at her. "I've had enough of these cruel games you play with him. He's on the edge and you're just clever enough to keep him teetering there."

Shalane handed the check to him. He began to snicker and she looked at him quizzically. "He didn't even sign it, Shalane. It isn't worth a dime to you or anyone else. Why don't you take it home and frame it. A reminder of how good you could have had it." He turned sharply and walked away.

Shalane remained in the doorway, still shocked by the

realization that Mason's signature was not on the check. She watched Julian's car speed out of the parking lot. She was not done with them yet, either of them.

Mason had taken a shower and was able to wash the scent of Shalane from his hands, but not from his mind. He sat in his bathrobe in front of the fireplace. Cassidy gave him a small glass of whiskey, but then locked the liquor cabinet. She watched him for a long time, imagining him with a son or daughter all his own to love. He'd be just like their father had been. Warm, gentle and understanding.

"I'm glad we found each other, Mason. It must have been the right time for all this to happen," she said brushing his hair back.

He attempted a smile for her benefit, but the tears were beginning to show in his eyes again. "Shalane is not something I want to share with you, Cassie."

"I know, but maybe she is something you can talk to me about. Something I can understand, or at least try to. I can listen, even if I don't have any answers for you. How long have you needed me? Has it been as long as I've needed you?" she asked.

He tried again to smile for her, this time the tears flowed freely. He gently placed his hand on the side of her face, and she covered it with her own. He gently kissed her forehead and hugged her fiercely.

Julian entered the den and sat beside Cassidy. He and Mason had been friends far too long to let each other get hurt or be destroyed. Mason looked as bewildered as he had felt the previous week. It was difficult to believe that the events of the last week had not taken place over several months. Julian shook his head and lit a cigarette. He could kick himself for not putting an end to Shalane and her games a long time ago. She had been nothing but trouble from day one. If only Mason had not been so blindly in love with her, and had rarely experienced that kind of intimacy before. Even Shalane was better than having no one.

CHAPTER FOUR

A few weeks later Mason and Julian released a new album. The first single was rising steadily up the charts, and things were finally returning to normal. Cassidy spent long, patient hours listening to them practice. Some practices lasted all night and she would fall asleep waiting for Julian to return home. Her days were filled with painting and shopping. Cassidy had a talent with paint and a canvas, but she was careful not to let it interfere with the precious little free time she had with Julian. It didn't bother her that Julian was so busy, as long as she was sure that he loved her and could make time for them to be alone occasionally.

Cassidy was working on a large canvas in the studio that had been set up for her when Julian walked in. "Let's go out tonight," he said.

"I thought you and Mason had a meeting tonight?" she replied, smiling as he kissed the side of her neck.

"He said he could handle it without me. He wants us to spend some time together."

"Well, dinner sounds good to me," she said, turning to clean her brushes. "What did you have in mind?"

"Marriage. I thought you and I would run away and get married tonight. What do you think, Cass?" he asked as he handed her a beautiful diamond and sapphire ring.

Cassidy was speechless. She was facing the sink when

he asked the question. Now she turned and stared at him through tear filled eyes. Julian was concerned until she came to him, put her arms around him and held him close.

"It's beautiful, Jule. I don't know what to say," she whispered against his chest.

"Say yes, say you'll marry me," he replied.

"There's nothing I want more than to be your wife," she said, looking up into his eyes. "I've never been so happy."

Julian swung her around and gently set her back on her feet. He then took the ring and slipped it onto her finger. She smiled brightly, her eyes dancing as he caressed her cheek. She kissed him long and deeply.

"You get dressed and I'll make the reservation. I'll be back to get you in an hour. Will that be long enough?" he asked.

"I'll be waiting for you," she said. He turned to leave. "Julian?"

"Yes," he replied.

"I love you so much," she smiled.

"I love you, too. You've just made me feel as if I could walk on air," Julian stated dreamily. "I'll be back in an hour." He left to make the final arrangements.

Mason sat at his desk talking on the telephone when Julian came in holding a bottle of champagne and wearing a boyish grin. Mason shook his head and smiled, he finished up his call and placed the receiver back in its cradle. Julian placed a glass in front of him and popped the cork on the champagne before settling into his own chair in front of the desk.

"What's the occasion?" Mason asked.

"You will be happy to know that I have just asked your

beautiful sister to marry me and she has accepted." Julian filled their glasses and made a short toast to happiness. Mason's smile began to fade. "We were going to run away tonight, but it wouldn't be the same without you. Do you think you could give her away, and still be my best man?" Julian continued.

Mason ran his hand through his hair and set his glass down without taking a sip. He swiveled his chair to look out the window at the evening sky and sighed, "You haven't thought this through, have you?

"I thought it would be better if I didn't. Why? What's wrong?" Julian sipped his champagne, the grin replaced by a look of puzzlement.

"What kind of life can you give her? We are getting ready to begin a world tour. We will be gone for six months or more. Are you planning to bring her with us? Will she even want to join us on the road? The ride on that tour bus for days on end is bad enough for us. You should know how short everyone's fuses get from being cooped up. It's not the kind of life I want for my sister. She deserves to be in the light, Jule. She needs to pursue her own talents and become a star in her own right. How can you say you love her, and want to keep her locked up in a tour bus?"

Julian smiled and half laughed, "You are either trying to make me feel nervous or feel guilty. I'm sorry but it won't work. I am sure of our love, and I can't feel guilty for falling in love with her. She is the best thing that has ever happened to me, and she is just as in love with me. Why are you trying to undermine this?"

"The question should be, why are you doing this? If you

really think about it, you will realize that this isn't right, this life won't make her happy. You can't give her a stable life with your career. I don't want to see either of you hurt. She's already been through enough because I wasn't there to take care of her," Mason said, matter-of-factly.

Julian rose from his chair, and took another cigarette from his pack. He carefully considered what Mason had said. He had been so happy when he arrived, now he felt as if his heart had been ripped from his chest. What if Mason was right? How could he fix it, without hurting Cassidy?

"What do you want me to do? She's already said yes, Mason. She's getting ready to go right now. I can't very well walk in and tell her that I've arbitrarily changed my mind. I meant every word I said to her tonight, she'll see right through me."

"Just go away, Julian, far away for a long time. Let her get over you," Mason said.

"You can't be serious, Mason. I couldn't possibly hurt her like that. She would be devastated. Do you really think I could be that heartless?" Julian stared at him in disbelief.

"She'll get over it. I'll be here for her," Mason said simply.

"What about me? How am I supposed to get over her? I am in love with her."

"Then you'll take my advice. You won't marry her and make her miserable. With the lives we lead, we can't possibly make a marriage work."

Julian was stunned by the smoothness with which Mason seemed to have taken control of his life. He left the room without saying another word. He drove for hours going no place in particular. He finally headed for home.

Meanwhile, Cassidy sat on her bed pretending to read. She glanced at the clock each time she finished a paragraph. Actually she had read the same paragraph so often she had lost count. She was beginning to worry.

Julian finally returned looking exhausted and confused. Cassidy reached for the bag she had packed, but Julian began to undress and headed to the bathroom. He slipped into bed saying nothing. Sensing that something was wrong Cassidy didn't ask any questions. She marked her place and set her book and glasses on her nightstand. She went into the bathroom to get ready for bed herself. She slipped in beside Julian and cuddled up next to him. She softly kissed his chest, and reached up to caress his cheek. She was glad that he had come home safe.

"What happened to dinner?" she asked.

"I couldn't get away after all. I'm sorry that I didn't call," he replied. He turned off the lamp before taking her in his arms. She could feel him tremble as he pulled her close.

"What's wrong?"

"Nothing," he replied, too quickly.

"Come on, Jule. I know you better than that."

"Cassidy, I just missed you, and I feel badly for upsetting you. That's all." He tried to smile in the dark and reached out to trace the familiar curve of her cheek with his fingers.

He pressed kisses to her face and the rest of her as well. Gently tracing every line of her body as he memorized her beauty. Cassidy never questioned the depth of their passion that night, only returned whatever he had to give and enjoyed the feelings of love they shared. Julian almost frightened her at the same time, acting as if they were doing this for the last time. His kisses were so thorough and hungry, as he urged her to their own private paradise. His fingers curled into her amber hair and pulled her head back so he could kiss her neck, trailing down to the valley of her firm, bare breasts.

Julian left her breathless, gasping between kisses. She began to ache with a need for him, long before his teasing ascended to a level of passion greater than they had ever achieved before. He was trying to reach her the only way he could think of. When at last he gave himself fully to her, plunging into the warmth that generated between her thighs. She arched her back to receive him and moaned in delight as the waves began to crash over her. Suddenly they were floating, up with the clouds, then the stars. As they reached the peak of their passion he began to whisper her name over and over again, until they could move no more, and slowly returned to earth. As they drifted off to sleep, Cassidy's only thoughts were of the years ahead, and the life they would build as man and wife.

CHAPTER FIVE

The early morning breeze woke Cassidy from her deep sleep. She tried to focus away from the bright sun shining through the windows. Then she sighed, and turned to take her lover again in her arms, but found only his empty pillows. She sat up, rubbed the sleep from her eyes and began to get out of bed when she saw a note and single white rose on the nightstand. She smiled as she held the note to her nose before she read it and smelled the familiar scent of Julian's cologne.

Dearest Cassidy,

I thought a lot about my proposal while I was away last night. Nothing has or ever will make me happier than your acceptance. I want you to believe that I will always love you more than I could ever tell you.

Forgive me for thinking I could make you happy when we both know my career would only get in the way. It hurts to leave you like this. Even as I watch you sleep while I write these words I am struck by how angelic you look.

You'll get over me somehow and find a man who can be all you need him to be, and have the family that you have always dreamed of. Thank you so much for these last months. You have taught me what true love is and how beautiful it can be.

Julian

Cassidy felt a cold knot of fear in her stomach as she stumbled from their bed and ran to the closet. She closed her eyes and said a brief prayer before she opened the doors. She gasped; everything of Julian's was gone. His dresser was empty as well. She could hardly see through her tears as she struggled to dress herself and went to the garage, pulling her hair back into a messy ponytail as she went. His car was gone as well. Her head began to reel as she tried desperately to comprehend what had happened between last night and this morning. Cassidy went to Mason's office in the studio. She slammed the door closed when she entered, startling him. He could see the anger on face and the tears in her eyes.

"Tell me where he is, Mason!"

"Cassie, it will be better this way. Believe me, he is only trying to do what will be best for you," he said calmly, rising from his chair. He came to where she was standing and reached to embrace her. Without even thinking about it, she reached up and slapped him.

"Don't patronize me, Mason. I want to know where he has gone, and I want to know now. I am not playing games!" she said, struggling to maintain some sense of composure.

"I can't tell you, Cassie. I promised him that I would not," Mason stated, while he rubbed the red mark that was forming on his cheek.

"I don't care. I don't care about your promise and I don't care how difficult the future may be. I know what kind of commitment we were going to make. Julian means everything to me. He is my future. Don't you understand that?" Her tears were beginning to flow anew, and her anger was beginning to build. "I don't understand either of you. What makes the two of you think you need to make my decisions for me? I'm perfectly capable of knowing what I want and need. Now, tell me where he is Mason, or I'll — "

At that moment Julian entered the office and interrupted her, "Cassidy, I'm right here. Don't take this out on Mason."

Cassidy stared at him in disbelief, and then ran to him. "I knew you wouldn't leave me."

Julian shook his head. "I'm sorry but I am leaving. There are a few things here that I need to pick up." Julian gently pushed her away and walked past her. She turned to Mason, the confusion painfully obvious in her eyes. She followed Julian as he left the office, still not believing that this was really happening. She caught up with him in the garage, where his car was loaded with bags. She caught his arms, but he wouldn't look at her. She hesitated before releasing him.

"Jule, please, you don't have to go. I know we can get through whatever the future holds. I would never interfere with your career. All I care about is you and our love," she said gently.

"Maybe not now, but eventually you will care, Cassidy. Sooner or later you will want to start a family. I don't have time for those things, you would have to do it all by

50

yourself. The only people I have time for are strangers. You would resent me for not being there when you need me," he said evenly.

Cassidy stared at him, feeling as if he had slapped her. "You don't love me, do you? You obviously don't know me."

"If you don't let me go now, I will leave when the first opportunity arises. I will wait until you've gone shopping, or you are sleeping. I will get away, Cassidy, and you can't stop me," he snapped.

"Then I won't sleep, I won't shop, I won't leave the house. What do you want me to say, what can I do?" she cried, desperately grasping for any shred of hope.

"Nothing, Cassidy, there is nothing you can say or do. It has to be this way." He turned and opened his car door. He couldn't look her in the face, he was afraid she would see the real truth in his eyes. More than that, he didn't want to see the pain he knew would be in hers.

He got into the car and pulled the door shut, but not before she could say, "I love you."

He stared hard at his steering wheel, and said, "That will change, I'm not coming back, Cassidy." He started the engine and slammed it into gear, his tires squealing as he pulled out of the garage, and out of her life.

Cassidy collapsed and began to sob uncontrollably. It had to be a terrible nightmare. Any moment now she would awaken to Julian's soothing voice and the haven of his arms. She did feel arms around her, but turned to find Mason kneeling beside her. She shoved him away angrily, and told him to leave her alone.

She replayed the last 24 hours in her mind, trying to

find the answer. What had gone wrong? How could they have been so blissfully happy last night and be here now? They were so in love, she was sure of it. Now he was gone, and was angry with her for trying to stop him.

She got into her car and fumbled for her keys. She could hardly see to drive, but she couldn't stay at the house any longer. She certainly didn't want to spend any time in the room where they had made such incredible love the night before. She tried to shake the memory and clear her mind. She drove until she finally gained some measure of control over her tears, and then returned to the house. She couldn't call it home anymore without Julian. She pulled up to the door and left the engine running and the door open. She didn't care if it ran out gas, or overheated. All she wanted was to be alone with her thoughts and her pain. She fell asleep crying on the sofa.

When she awoke, she looked around the room. Everything here reminded her of Julian. She still could not believe he had done this. The ache in her heart was so intense the pain was almost physical. Still, she couldn't bring herself to hate him, not even close.

Mason tried to see her, but she wouldn't let him in. She wouldn't have even been able to talk to him anyway. She still felt as if she was trapped in a nightmare. The more she thought about it, the more she felt Mason was somehow to blame. She slept, and awakened time after time to the same awful realization. Nothing had changed, Julian was still gone, and she was still waiting for him to return. Instead of getting easier, it only became more painful, but she didn't or couldn't hate him.

Two months later she threw herself back into her art.

She aired out her studio, and went on a shopping spree for new art supplies. She began a list of local galleries where she could display her work. Slowly she began to live again.

One evening she ventured into the studio. She had not spoken to Mason in the last two months. She didn't even know if he had gone on the scheduled tour. He was playing his piano when she entered and didn't even notice her presence for several minutes. She listened to him patiently waiting for him to finish the piece he was playing. He looked up and smiled at her, grateful that she had come to see him. He turned on the piano bench so that he was facing her.

"Hey stranger."

"Hey," she replied, returning his smile.

"How are you, Cassie? Are you all right?" he asked.

"Not yet, but I will be, someday," she replied wistfully. "I'm so sorry, Mason, for the way I've acted towards you. It wasn't fair.

"I suppose if one man acts like swine, then we all become swine, for a while anyway," he teased.

Cassidy laughed, relieved that he had accepted her apology so gracefully. He hugged her, and she didn't push him away, instead leaning into his shoulder as the tears began to flow. "I just need to know one thing, Mason," she sniffed. "I need to know if he is OK. Can you tell just that much?"

"He's fine, Cassie. He's just fine."

"Oh God, I miss him so much, Mason," she managed to say between hitching sobs.

"It will be all right, Cassidy. I promise you. All you

have to do is let him go, stop revisiting all of your memories," he advised, stroking her hair. "It's easier said than done though, believe me, I know."

CHAPTER SIX

The first week of December, Mason introduced his sister to a friend of his. Roman Spencer was an attractive man in his mid-thirties. He was a few inches taller than Cassidy, his skin was fair and his hair was dusty brown. Roman was very charming with a good sense of humor, and by coincidence he owned the most popular gallery in London. Cassidy was relieved to learn that she could still enjoy herself, it was good to laugh again. She found that she and Roman had a lot in common, but she knew that Mason had set them up.

Roman was serious about his art and he appreciated genuine talent. He wasted no time in establishing a studio for Cassidy in his gallery. There she could work in peace without distraction. Roman would drop in occasionally to admire her progress. He wouldn't say anything, only walk from piece to piece nodding his head. They struck a deal for an exhibit of her work to open after the beginning of the new year. She knew that Roman's interest in her was sincere, but she was uneasy at the prospect of a new relationship. The wounds Julian had inflicted on her heart were not yet healed. It was going to be difficult disappointing Mason, he held high hopes for she and Roman. She did make an attempt to let Roman wine and dine her and did find herself becoming quite fond of him.

Roman was captivated by Cassidy's beauty; he wanted

desperately to replace her memories of Julian with new ones of their own. He loved to watch her when she was working. The light in the studio seemed to bring out fire in her auburn hair, and deepened the sapphire blue of eyes, he felt as if he could drown in their depths. She smiled brightly when he entered the studio, and it warmed his heart. He knew that she had not had much to smile about recently.

He stood in the doorway watching her now. "How's it coming today, Cassidy?" he asked.

She jumped slightly; she had been so involved in the piece she was working on that she didn't even notice that he had come in. "You scared me," she said with a sigh.

"I'm sorry," he smiled. "I didn't mean to."

"In answer to your question, I am doing fine. Actually, I was just finishing for the night. I would like to come do some touchups in morning, if you don't mind."

"That would be fine. I was wondering if maybe you'd like to have dinner with me?" he asked.

"It's pretty late, do you think that we could find someplace still open?" she wondered.

"I'm sure we can, though it might not be very elegant, mind you."

"I'm in the mood for a cheap burger and greasy fries anyway," she said with a smile.

"Whatever you want. I'll wait for you in the car," he said on his way out.

Cassidy looked around the small diner they had chosen; they were sitting in a corner booth. She took a cigarette from her purse and began to search for a lighter among its contents. Roman lit the cigarette for her and slipped his gold lighter back into his pocket without a word. She smiled and thanked him, then looked up as the waitress approached with menus.

"Can I get you something to drink while you decide?" she asked.

"Yes, a diet cola, please," Cassidy replied.

"I think I'll have coffee, no cream," said Roman.

They looked at the menus in silence and then set them on the table when they had decided. Cassidy looked at the jukebox that had caught her eyes earlier. She bit her lip pensively, and then nodded as if she had made up her mind. She asked Roman to order for her, then made her way to the jukebox. She returned in a few minutes, saying nothing. The music she had selected filled the small diner.

"What is this you've played?" Roman asked, wrinkling his nose slightly.

"I take it you're not a huge fan of rock-n-roll," she said, laughing. "How long have you known my brother?"

"Quite awhile. We went to college together."

"This is him singing," Cassidy replied, laughing again.

"Is that so? I guess you wouldn't be interested in something a little more classical, right?" he asked.

"Oh no! I've never seen an orchestral concert or the opera, but I am familiar with a lot of the music."

"I'll have to see about taking you to the opera one evening," he suggested, with a wink.

"I'll look forward to it," she said, returning his wink.

A few weeks later, Cassidy's big day arrived. Her exhibit opened to critical acclaim. Mason arrived fashionably late, with a beautiful blonde on his arm. Cassidy excused herself from the small group of admirers that surrounded her and made her way through the crowd to Mason and his companion.

"Mason, I am so glad that you could make it." She gave him a brief hug and a quick kiss on the cheek.

He returned the hug and kiss and introduced her to his date. "Cassidy, this is Lacey Lee, Lacey, this is my beautiful, talented sister Cassidy."

"It's so nice to finally meet you, Cassidy. Mason has told me so much about you. He has been so excited about this exhibit," Lacey said.

"I think he has been looking forward to it more than I have lately," Cassidy teased.

Lacey laughed and Cassidy showed them around the gallery. Roman joined them, looking a little nervous. He came from the champagne fountain, holding two glasses. He handed a glass to Cassidy and shook Mason's hand.

"Can I see you for a moment, Mason?" They excused themselves from the ladies and retreated to Roman's office.

"Why all the secrecy, Roman?" Mason asked.

"Actually, I have two things to tell you. First of all, there have been some very generous offers made on Cassidy's paintings."

"And that is a problem?" Mason said, curiously. He still didn't understand why Roman seemed so uneasy.

"No," Roman answered him. He reached into his pocket and withdrew a small velveteen box. "But this may be," he hesitated, clearing his throat. "I want to marry your sister, Mason. Do I have your blessing?"

Mason lifted his champagne glass and tapped it against the rim of the one that Roman was holding. "Without a doubt, I do believe that you should be asking Cassidy," he said, placing his free hand on Roman's shoulder. They returned to the party.

A short while later Roman moved to the front of the gallery and stood beside an easel, which held a large canvas concealed with a drape.

"Ladies and gentlemen, may I have your attention for a moment please. Cassidy, love, would you come here, please. I want to show you something."

Cassidy smiled at him and made her way through the crowd. Roman had been keeping a secret for weeks, maybe now she would find out what it was. He took her hand and kissed her cheek, and then with a grand gesture he pulled the drape from the canvas. There on the canvas, in bright colors, were the words: "Marry me, Cassidy, I love you."

Cassidy was stunned, all she could do was stare. The silence was heavy around them as everyone waited for her answer. Her mind drifted for a moment, back to the evening that Julian had asked her the same question. She could feel the tears beginning to build in her eyes. There had only been two men in her life, Julian and now Roman. She nodded her head and turned to face him.

"I'd be a fool if I didn't, wouldn't I?" There was a collective sigh of relief from the crowd watching them. Mason was smiling broadly as Roman took the ring from its box and slipped on her finger.

"Oh God, Cassidy, I am so in love with you." Roman gently wiped the tears from her face, staring into her eyes before slipping the ring onto her finger, where it came to rest on the ring that Julian had given her a lifetime ago.

They embraced and kissed as if they were the only two people in the room. A round of applause from the crowd brought them back to earth.

Later that evening, alone on the balcony, Cassidy gazed at the brightly lit fountain in the courtyard between the house she now lived in and the house she had shared with Julian. Absentmindedly, she played with the rings on her finger, lost in her reverie. At last she removed both of them and placed Roman's ring back, alone. She found herself captivated by the sapphire ring and felt tears begin to burn again. She shook away the painful memories and entered her bedroom. She walked to her dresser and opened her jewelry box, but couldn't bring herself to drop the ring in. She caught her reflection in the mirror; she was still wearing the peach gown from the gala that evening. Quickly she changed into a pair of jeans and an oversized shirt that Julian had left behind.

Cassidy arrived at the dark, deserted studio and took a deep breath before entering. She used her key to get into Julian's office; she wasn't a fool, she knew that he was here daily with Mason. She didn't know where he was living though. His cologne was heavy in air, and the ashtray was overflowing with cigarette butts. She saw his jacket draped over the back of a chair and picked it up, slipping it on and pulling it tight around her. She curled up in his chair and closed her eyes. The memories came flooding back, his smile, his scent, his touch and his kiss.

Slowly she opened her eyes and spoke to the memories, "It's time to let you go, Jule. If I don't do this, I can never love Roman the way I should. We will never be truly happy, and I won't allow that. I do love him, it will never be the same as my love for you, but it is enough." She slipped his ring out of her pocket and onto the third finger on her right hand.

Early the next morning Julian entered his office to find Cassidy sound asleep in his chair. He stood and watched her for a long time, feeling his heart breaking all over again. Finally he turned and left quietly so that he wouldn't wake her.

When Mason arrived at his office, Julian was sitting on the sofa, waiting for him. Mason smiled broadly at his friend and patted him on the back. "Guess what?"

"What?" Julian replied, soberly.

"Roman asked Cassidy to marry him last night. Isn't that wonderful?" he laughed.

"Yeah, just wonderful. I am so happy for her and for you. But, did you know that — " He was cut short as Cassidy entered the room.

"Mason, I …" she choked on what she was about to say as she noticed Julian sitting there.

"Hello, Cass," he said, trying to hide the pain he felt.

"Cassie, what are you doing here?" Mason asked.

"Mason … Hello, Julian. Mason, I … I gotta go. I'm sorry." She ran from the room.

Julian turned to stare at Mason before going after her. He caught up with her in the garage, frantically searching her pockets for her car keys. He gently took her arm and felt her stiffen under his touch. She shook his hand from her arm before turning to look at him.

"What do you want, Julian?" She wiped at the tears that were running down her cheeks.

"I'm sorry, Cass," he said simply.

"Yeah. I'm sure you are. So am I," she said sharply. "Is that all? Am I free to go now, or was there something else you wanted?"

Yes, there was something else he wanted. He wanted to take her in his arms, kiss her and tell her how much he still loved her. He wanted to hold her until everything was right between them again. It crushed him to see her tearstained cheeks, to know how much it was torturing both of them to be standing here like this, after so many months. Instead of telling her all this, he merely sighed and shook his head.

He turned away as he said, "Congratulations. All my best to you and Roman, I wish you every happiness." He continued back to the studio, leaving her to stare after him.

Mason watched as Julian stormed into his office, slamming the door behind him hard enough to rattle the windows. Carefully Mason followed, and found Julian staring at the wall.

"Mason, the last thing I need right now is more of your advice. If I had listened to my heart instead of you I would be her husband now. Obviously, I was not good enough for her, ironically Roman Spencer seems to be. I just can't believe it. I suggest you show yourself out, now." Julian struggled to control his anger and frustration.

"Now, just a minute — " Mason started.

"No, no more minutes, you don't control me, Mason. Get out!" he yelled.

CHAPTER SEVEN

Cassidy and Roman returned from their honeymoon in Europe and began their search for the perfect home. When they found it she began to pack the things that remained at Julian's house. She walked through the house one last time reliving all of the memories that had been created there. It was a beautiful home, but it would never belong to she and Roman, it would always be Julian's house.

After two years Roman made Cassidy a full partner in his gallery. Together they expanded it to make room for new and better artists. Cassidy became well respected and known, not only for her talent as an artist, but as a businesswoman as well.

Mason and Julian toured the United States and worked their way back through Europe. Mason and Lacey were becoming quite serious and spent a lot of time together when the tour was over. Cassidy and Lacey became very close friends. Cassidy was overjoyed that Mason had found such a good woman.

Mason and Julian kept in contact regularly, but Cassidy had not seen, or heard from him, in five years. Not since the morning she had fallen asleep in his office. Mason was very careful, and never brought him up in any of their conversations. If the discussion should turn to him, Mason would quickly change the subject.

Cassidy and Roman planned a large dinner party to

celebrate their upcoming wedding anniversary. She stayed home from the gallery on the day of the celebration to help put the finishing touches on decorations, and make final decisions on the menu. Roman arrived home and set his briefcase on the table in the foyer, and gathered her in his arms.

"Happy anniversary, darling." He planted a kiss on her lips.

"Happy anniversary to you, too, love," she smiled.

"How many are on the guest list for tonight?" Roman asked, after setting her carefully back on her feet.

"Ten. Why?" she asked, tossing some extra streamers into the trash.

"Well … now, we have twelve. And, the extras are a surprise, so don't ask," he smiled.

"Tell me," Cassidy said, chewing on her bottom lip.

"If I tell you, it won't be a surprise anymore, now will it? And don't try asking Mason either."

"He knows?" she asked, beginning to pout.

"Yes, he does."

"Can I have a hint?"

"No," Roman said, his eyes beginning to sparkle.

"Party-pooper," Cassidy whined. "I've got to drop off Mason's suit. Lacey asked me to pick it up, since she began working double shifts at the hospital, her time is at a minimum."

"If she didn't love being a nurse so much, I'd suggest she quit. That woman works much too hard," Roman grumbled.

"Well … I'll be back in an hour. Love you," Cassidy called over her shoulder as she left.

Mason was on the phone when she came in with his suit. As she hung it on the doorknob, he smiled and motioned her in. She sat down and began to straighten the papers that were scattered on his desk. He quickly finished his call and replaced the receiver. He covered her hands with his own and began to slowly shake his head. He led her gently to the other side of the desk and sat her in another chair. He sat in his chair and lit a cigarette.

"Why must you insist my desk be clean?"

"You should be organized."

"Cassidy, why do you think I have an accountant?" he laughed. "I can't even balance my checkbook."

"I have some news for you," Cassidy said, changing the subject.

"Well, what is it?" Mason leaned forward.

"You're going to be an uncle," she replied calmly, leaning forward until her nose almost touched his.

Mason began to reach for a cigarette, and then shook his head, as if he thought better of it. A grin began to spread over his face, until his eyes were even smiling.

"Really?" Cassidy nodded. "How's Roman taking this news of yours?" Mason asked.

"I told him this morning. It was my anniversary gift to him. He's nervous as hell. Of course, he will probably embarrass me at dinner tonight when he tells everyone."

"I'm so excited for the two of you. Congratulations," Mason said, as she stood and reached for her purse. He kissed her cheek as she turned to leave.

"Oh," Cassidy said, looking at her watch, "I told him I'd be back in an hour, so I have to get going. I'll see you at seven thirty."

"OK," he said, still smiling broadly.

As the doorbell rang and the guests began arriving, Cassidy took the spiraling steps two at a time. Roman caught her around the waist as she reached the bottom and gently swung her to the floor. She looked dazzling in a lavender gown that hugged her hourglass figure. As he let her go she began to straighten his tie.

"You never do get this right," she teased him.

"Maybe that is why I married you," he smiled.

She pouted at him for a moment before she began to fuss at her hair and slowly turn around in front of him. "What do you think? Should I go change?" she asked, coyly.

"No, you've taken my breath away just as you are. Besides, you've already changed three times this evening," he reminded her.

"If you're sure … when is the surprise coming?"

"As soon as your brother gets here."

Roman spun her around as the butler led in another couple. He paused in front of them and announced, "Jason and Kelly Peters." Jason and Kelly congratulated them before following the other guests into the party.

"Manuel and Tanja Cartier. Cameron and Tabitha Sears," the butler read their names as he took their invitations. "George and Jordanna Davenport." Roman shook George's hand. They had been friends, as well as business associates, for years. Mason had introduced them after George had expressed an interest in using Roman's artwork for his album jackets.

Jordan leaned in to kiss Cassidy's cheek and congratulate her. "You look wonderful, marriage obviously agrees with you."

"You too, Jordan," Cassidy smiled.

"Mason Manis and Miss Lacinda Lee," the butler read.

Lacey blushed, "Lacey," she corrected him.

Cassidy laughed and the two women embraced. "Julian Drake and Miss Rachelle Winters."

Cassidy looked up quickly at the sound of his name. She felt her face flush as she caught sight of him for the first time in over five years. The tan suit he wore appeared to have been custom-made for him, a simple white shirt completing the effect. His chestnut hair was neatly layered away from his handsome face. He was laughing at something Mason had said, and hadn't noticed her yet.

The woman with him was tall and slender, and appeared to be in her mid-twenties. Her copper hair was pulled back into a French tuck, leaving some loose curls to frame her pretty face.

Julian held out his arm to Rachelle, who took it with an adoring smile. Cassidy felt a pang of jealousy and prayed that he would not be able to see it. She gazed at the floor while she fought to regain her composure, finally looking up to meet his eyes. He nodded and stepped up to take her hands in his and leaned down to kiss her cheek. He still wore the same cologne, and the familiar scent brought a fresh rush of heat to her face. The room began to swim and she felt lightheaded. She shook her head trying to clear it, when the room began to fade to shades of gray, then black.

"Cassie!" Mason and Roman cried in unison as they rushed to take her from Julian's arms.

He had swept her up as she collapsed to keep her head from striking the floor.

"Oh God, is she all right?" Lacey quickly crossed the room and led them to the den. She had them lay her on the couch and placed a pillow under her head. She sent Mason for some cool water and a cloth while patting Cassidy's cheeks gently, trying to rouse her. Lacey assured Roman that Cassidy would be fine and sent him to tend to the guests. He hesitated a moment before he went to show the guests to the dining table. Mason and Lacey stayed with Cassidy until she awoke. She appeared disoriented and sat up quickly.

"She's all right, Mason. You stay with her for a minute, and I'll meet you in the dining room when she is ready," Lacey smiled reassuringly as she rose to join the party.

"Thank you," Mason said.

"What happened?" Cassidy asked, pressing her hand to her forehead.

"You fainted, darling. You'll be all right. How do you feel?" Mason asked.

"A little dizzy still. Mason, I thought I saw Julian, isn't that strange?" She smiled at him as she swung her legs over the edge of the couch.

"No, you did see him. He's here. Roman invited him. Julian is your surprise."

"Oh my God, no. Please tell me that I am dreaming. He's really here?" she asked.

"Yes, I'm afraid he is," Mason replied as he helped her get up. He watched with concern as she went to a mirror to check her hair and make-up. He heard her whisper Julian's name as she fixed a curl. "Cassie, if you want I'll ask him to leave. I am sure he will understand. I know he will," he said, as he wiped fresh tears off of her cheeks.

"No," she shook her head. "I can't ask him to leave in front of all the guests. I can handle this. The past is the past, and I have a wonderful future ahead of me."

Mason rubbed her arms, and looked into her face to see if she was truly as confident as she was trying to sound. There was something in her eyes that had not been there in a very long time.

"I know you can handle it, the point is you don't have to. If you change your mind, don't be afraid to let me know, OK?"

"OK," she said, taking one last look at her reflection. "Shall we?" she asked, extending her arm for Mason.

Everyone was seated at the long, elegant table. They smiled when Mason and Cassidy entered the room, arm in arm. He escorted her to her seat at the end of the table, and pulled her chair out for her. Roman smiled warmly at her, much relieved. The conversation picked up again. Everyone seemed to be getting along well. Cassidy let her gaze drift around the table until it inevitably fell upon Julian, who was seated to her right.

"You look stunning, Cass," he said, as he raised his glass to her. Everyone at the table agreed with his observation.

Roman came to stand behind her. "She looks more stunning than ever this evening, don't you think?" He placed his hand on her shoulder as he announced, "But then, don't all expectant mothers take on an unusual glow?" It took a moment for everyone to realize what he meant. Then the table erupted with congratulations and handshakes, as Cassidy blushed under all of the attention. "Quite the anniversary gift, wouldn't you say?" Roman beamed.

As the congratulations continued, Cassidy felt a pair of eyes bore into her soul. She looked up to see Julian staring at her; he took her hand and tried to make his congratulations sound sincere. The pain in his eyes was obvious to her, and the words rang hollow and false. She quickly excused herself after a toast to the happy couple and left the room. Roman frowned as she left and began to go after her.

Julian caught his arm, "Let me go talk to her, Roman, please. I am sure that I am what is wrong." Roman hesitated, but agreed to let him have a moment with her.

The door to the bedroom was slightly ajar, and he could hear her sobs as he came to the top of the stairs. He knocked lightly on the door before entering the room. Cassidy sat up and gazed out of the window. He closed the door, and leaned against it. The silence was heavy and awkward, but he didn't know what to say.

Without looking at him Cassidy asked, "Why did you come?"

"I wanted to see you happy, Cassidy. I didn't think it would hurt you to see me after all this time," he replied.

"It does hurt, Julian, it will always hurt. I only wish you hurt half as much as I do. I had almost forgotten the knife that was lodged in my heart, until you arrived to give it another good twist." She began to cry again.

"I'm so sorry, Cassidy. That is truly the last thing I wanted to do. I'll go, I have always been a fool where you are concerned."

"Jule," she cried and turned, panic in her voice.

"I shouldn't have come." He trembled as he stood at the

door, his hand poised to turn the knob, yet not wanting to leave. "I didn't want to bring you pain."

Cassidy ran to him and he turned to catch her in an embrace that should have been long forgotten. To feel her so close to him was a gift he wasn't worthy of, but he held anyway. Once again seeing her cry, and hearing her whisper his name over and over, reawakened the ache in his own heart. He held her face in his hands, futilely wiping at her tears with his thumbs. She felt him tremble and saw the tears begin to well in his eyes. No words could express what they felt as their lips met, in a kiss that lit a passion that neither of them had felt in years.

Julian broke the kiss and held her tight to his chest, breathless with the memory of how it had been between the two of them. He stroked her hair, and inhaled her perfume. Cassidy listened to his heartbeat, and remembered falling asleep listening to it. She held him tighter, afraid that if she spoke the moment would shatter. This is what had been missing for the last five years. The emptiness was gone now.

She slowly looked up into his eyes, afraid of what she may see there. He leaned down to kiss her again as he swept her up in his embrace and effortlessly carried her to the bed. He gently laid her there and held her close, never breaking the kiss. Suddenly he rose, shaking his head.

"I'm sorry, Cassidy, I can't do this. Roman is one of my best friends. You're carrying his child. I just can't ..." his voice trailed off.

Cassidy's anger flared as hotly as her passion had just moments before. She stood up and slapped his face, leaving a stinging red mark.

"How could you do this to me?" she screamed. "I loved you, Julian. I still do. Just get out!"

"Cass, I …" he couldn't finish.

Fresh tears filled her eyes and ran down her cheeks. "It could have been you. We could have had everything. This could be your child. But you threw it all away, and never even offered an explanation. Now after all this time, you return to open every wound that Roman has tried so hard to heal."

"I have to go," he said.

"Please, Julian, please don't leave me again. Julian Drake, if you walk out on me again …" she didn't finish her thought.

"If I hurt you again, it would crush me," he said, slipping out the door.

Cassidy stood there, not wanting to believe what had happened. She had had him in her arms again, only to have him walk out the door. She ran to the window, watching for him, hoping that she wouldn't see him leave. He did leave though, Rachelle was trying desperately to keep up with him. Cassidy watched through her tears as he got into his car, and screeched out of the driveway.

CHAPTER EIGHT

Roman found Cassidy still crying. He asked Lacey to stay with her, and went to extend his apologies to the guests that remained. When the last of them had left, he joined Mason in the den. He paced up and down in front of the couch where Mason sat smoking, and shaking his head.

"Roman, don't be angry with Julian. This was not his fault. I tried to tell you that inviting him was a bad idea. They never had a chance to resolve anything. There are still too many unanswered questions and 'what ifs' for both of them." Mason rose to pour each of them a scotch.

"I wasn't thinking at all. I thought it would please her to see him. I knew how much she loved him once," he sighed. "I just didn't realize how much she still does. Or how much he still loves her for that matter. I guess I was more concerned with showing off. I truly didn't mean to hurt either of them." He shook his head sadly as he reached for the scotch Mason offered.

"She will be all right, Roman. Lacey is with her now."

"She was so hysterical."

"Lacey will be able to calm her down. They have become very close friends. Don't worry," Mason reassured.

Roman looked up. "I can't help but worry, Mason. She and the baby are my whole life. I may have ruined everything with this foolishness."

Both men turned as Lacey entered the room, their eyes asking questions neither of them dared give voice to.

Lacey took a deep breath, "She is relaxing now. I am sure the baby will be fine, and so will she."

The three of them sat and exchanged small talk for a short while before Mason and Lacey left for the evening. Roman took a deep breath and one last look about the room. He steeled himself for whatever may happen and began to ascend the stairs.

Cassidy didn't even look up when he entered the room. He stood for a brief moment before closing the door and crossing to where she sat quietly rocking and gazing out the window.

He knelt before her, his eyes pleading for forgiveness. "Cassidy, it will be all right. I promise I will never let him hurt you again."

"How can you say that, Roman? You brought him here, if you cared at all, you never would have invited him."

"I truly didn't realize how much it would hurt you, Cassidy. I thought enough time had passed. I swear there is nothing more important than you and our baby. I'm so very sorry," he apologized, laying his head in her lap.

She stroked his hair absentmindedly. "I forgive you, Roman." She pulled him close and held him for a long time.

Meanwhile, across town, Julian stood on the balcony outside his bedroom. He had only recently began living in his house again. He stared down at the fountain in the courtyard between the two houses.

He could still smell her perfume throughout the bedroom, even on the sheets they had once slept on. They

74

had been washed several times so he knew it could only be his imagination, but it was still so vivid. He had eventually come to terms with this, and been able to settle in again. But tonight, the scent was stronger than ever. He could still taste the wine from her lips that evening. Without thinking he reached up to touch his lips, where only hours before he had felt her surrender to him.

"Oh, Cass, if I could only change things, I would do it all so differently." He gazed up at the full moon as he made his wish.

Several weeks later, Roman was taking advantage of the early morning sunlight that filled the studio at home, while Cassidy ate a light breakfast. She watched him doing what he loved most, and felt very content. The painting he was working on would soon be the centerpiece of a new display in their gallery. He felt her eyes on him and turned to smile at her.

"Good morning, sunshine. How are we feeling today?" he inquired.

"We are feeling just fine," she replied.

"I will be leaving for that seminar later today. Are you feeling well enough to join me?"

"How long will we be gone, Roman?" she asked.

"Only a couple of days."

"If I weren't so tired and nauseous all the time I'd love to go with you, Roman. I think we could use some time away, but ..." her voice trailed off.

"I understand, darling," Roman reassured her. "We will have lots of chances later on. Right now you should focus on being well, for both of you," he smiled.

"I have some work to do anyway. Mason has asked me

to come up with some new ideas for their album cover."

"Don't over do it," Roman stated. "I want you to take it easy."

"I will be careful. I'll go pack your suitcase, is there anything special you want?" she asked as she walked toward the door.

"Actually, what I want is to make love to you all morning, but I don't think we would both fit in my suitcase," he smiled.

"You'll have to catch me first," Cassidy teased, biting her bottom lip.

As he set down his brush and cloth she darted out the door and headed for the stairs. Roman caught up with her easily and swept her up in his arms. For the first time in weeks he heard her truly laugh. He carried her up the stairs and laid her across their bed. He kissed her neck gently as he began to loosen the strings that held her dressing gown closed. He lifted his head and gazed into her eyes. Her smile faded and her fingers caressed him. But it was not him she touched, or watched so intently, in her mind it was Julian. She traced his lips, and ran her other hand through his hair.

"I love you," he whispered into her ear as he bent again to trace the line of her jaw with tender kisses.

When he lifted his head to kiss her lips, the illusion was shattered. She saw that it was not Julian, but Roman. Her eyes flooded with tears and she looked away. Roman sat and rocked her as she cried. He tried to say the things she needed to hear, but could not seem to find the right words.

"I ... I want to talk to Mason," she sobbed.

"OK, I'll call him right away. Sshh."

Julian set down his guitar when the phone rang. The band had been joking around when they arrived. Mason had gone to the back room to find the sheet music for a new song he wanted to work on. Julian smiled and waved at the guys to be quiet as he answered the phone. "Hello."

"Julian, this is Roman, I need to speak with Mason right away. Is he there?"

"Yeah, somewhere. Is something wrong?" Julian asked.

"It's Cassidy, she's very upset and has asked for him."

"I'll send him right over."

Julian almost collided with Mason, who was returning to the studio. "Whoa there, where's the fire, Julian."

Julian ignored Mason's attempt at humor. "It's Cassidy, Mason. Roman called and said she is really upset. She asked to see you. Here are my keys, my car is parked in front of the rest."

Mason took the keys and headed out of the studio, over his shoulder he called to the band, "Go on home, guys, I don't know how long this will take."

"Mason?" Julian said.

Mason turned around, "Yeah."

"Nothing," Julian shook his head, and turned away.

Roman was waiting at the door when he arrived. He hurried up the stairs to the master bedroom and found Cassidy still huddled, crying in the middle of the bed. She looked up when she heard him enter. "Oh, Mason," she sobbed. He sat on the bed and held her, stroking her hair, waiting for this fresh torrent of tears to subside. When she was able to regain control, she sat up and looked at Mason. "I don't love him," she stated simply.

Mason knew who "him" was, and prepared himself for

this as best he could. "Cass, I'll have Julian move away. You and Roman could buy the house and fix it up however you like."

"Mason, it's not the house. Why do you think I moved out after he left? That house has memories of us all through it. Redecorating wouldn't get rid of them. I simply don't love Roman, and I'm not sure that I ever did." This last she said very slowly, and hung her head with guilt.

"Yes you do, Cassie, you're going to have his baby. Don't do this to him. He loves you. Are you strong enough to put him through the pain that you are so familiar with? Can you really throw this away? What about your child?" he asked.

"I don't know, Mason, I don't know. I only know what is in my heart. And it isn't Roman."

Mason was silent for a long time, and then he took his sister's face and looked into her eyes. "Julian still loves you, too. I could see it in his eyes when he told me you needed me. I've seen it in his eyes for a very long time," Mason sighed. "I swore to myself that I would never tell you."

Cassidy's eyes grew bright with hope. "Tell him, Mason, tell him that I still love him. Tell him that I ache for him when I am alone. Tell him that I never meant to hurt him …" She began to cry again.

Mason stood up, and ran his hands through her hair. Again he took her face in his hands but his glare was stern this time when she looked at him. "You listen to me, Cassidy Spencer, let him go. You are tearing yourself and your marriage apart. Let him go. Pull yourself together. Let yourself love Roman. Forget Julian, you have to."

Cassidy pushed his hands away from her face. "Why can't you understand?"

"Cassie, please," Mason pleaded.

"Get out!" She threw a pillow at him. "Just get … out."

Mason hesitated for a moment, and then turned and left the room. He knew too well that the only person she would listen to now was Julian. Whenever she was this upset, Julian seemed to be the only one who could calm her down. But Mason knew that Roman would never let Julian talk to her again.

CHAPTER NINE

Roman carried his suitcase to the car and locked it in the trunk. He waited for his wife to come out. She seemed better after Mason's visit. He felt secure knowing her brother was close by. Cassidy hugged him, and then kissed him long and hard. She waved as he pulled out of the drive.

Julian was up late that night. He sat in his den and listened to the stereo. All he could think about was Cassidy. Mason hadn't really told him anything, except that she would eventually be all right. Julian shook his head, he knew something was wrong, he could feel it. He sipped absently from a cup of tea that had been sitting long enough to be cool now. He heard a faint knock on the door.

"Come in," he called.

"Mr. Drake, sir? There's someone here to see you," his maid said.

Julian hesitated, he wasn't sure that he wanted visitors right now. Then he decided that a little distraction might not be such a bad idea. "Send them in," he stood but continued to stare into the fire.

"Yes, sir."

Cassidy stepped into the dimly lit den and the maid smiled at her discretely before she quietly closed the doors. Cassidy stood at the door and absorbed all she could while she waited for him to turn around. When he did finally turn around, he opened his arms to her and she ran to him. They held each other tightly, neither daring to speak for fear of shattering the moment.

At last Julian leaned back and looked at her. "I knew you would come. I've been waiting for you," he whispered, stroking her hair back from her face.

"How could I stay away?" she questioned. "I love you."

"Let me hold you, Cassidy. I've been waiting for this moment for so very long." His body shuddered as his tears came, soon they were crying together.

"Why, Julian, why did you leave? That's all I want to know."

"Because I couldn't give you the kind of life I wanted to. The kind of life Roman has given you," he answered.

"Do you honestly think that Roman has made me any happier than you could have?"

"I was wrong. I could have made you happy. I could have made myself happy. But, I listened to Mason, and he scared me into leaving you. I really believed that you would come to resent missing out on the things that you've achieved. So I left, believing I was doing the right thing, not realizing how much it would hurt you anyway," Julian paused, and took a deep breath. "After I left I had to deal with all my pain alone. I wanted to be with you, call you, but I made a promise, to myself and to Mason. I used to drive around where I knew you'd be, just so I could see you. The truth is that I was still in love with you, and couldn't let go. Cass, please forgive me for being such a fool. If I could go back I would," his voice faltered.

Cassidy went to where he stood and touched his tear

stained face. She kissed the trails the tears had left down his cheeks, and put her arms around him. They held each other for a very long time, whispering words of love and forgiveness. Their lips met again and again, longer and deeper each time. At last Julian could hold back no longer, he swept her in his arms and carried her up the stairs. The rain outside seemed to keep time with their lovemaking. They absorbed each moment of the other's pleasure. Carefully, slowly remembering their long buried passions. Like a sacred ritual, they finished together and fell into the satisfied slumber of dreams, at last fulfilled.

The morning light hit Julian like a slap to the face. It was bright and clear. He opened his eyes and sat up to rub the sleep from them. Cassidy lay close cuddled against him unclothed. So many mornings had passed when he ached to wake up to her beautiful profile and here she was.

Gently he ran his hand down her slightly swollen belly. A child was growing within her. A child that wasn't his. Still he loved her and watched her sleep, even as he cradled her in his arms and lap, pulling the sheets over them. Her amber hair cascaded over his arms and he smoothed it away from her face. If this were the last time they touched intimately he wanted it to last so he would always remember the perfect curves of her face.

She felt his hands caressing her belly and the smell of him filled her senses. Cassidy didn't want to disturb him. Roman had never held her like this, never kissed her like Julian was doing. Soft kisses he pressed to each of her fingers and to her cheek. When he touched her lips with his, she ran her hand up through his hair to return it.

Julian smiled at her, "Have you been awake all this

time?"

"Yes," she grinned back teasingly.

Julian shook his head in disbelief when she smiled. "I love you."

"I love you, too," she replied.

He kissed her again. Cassidy looked up at him for a long time, enjoying the way his eyes danced with laughter and happiness. She remembered the way a smile was always on his face when they were together. Now Julian seemed in deep thought.

"Jule, do you feel guilty now?" she asked without thinking.

Julian sat up, so his back was to her. She sat up and put her arms around his waist and rested her face against his back. His fingers laced between hers as he stared at the wall. "If I did, I wouldn't be here now."

"I knew you would say something like that. Say that you love me as much as I love you." She pressed a kiss to his bare skin.

"I do, Cassidy. More than anything in this world," he smiled. "But, it's too late for us, now. You have a life with Roman."

Cassidy got up and put his shirt on. His words were true, but they hurt like hell. She did have a life with Roman, almost a family. She started to walk past him, but he caught her arm and pulled her back to him quickly. He touched her face and took her hand in his. Julian held it to his chest so she could feel his heart beneath her fingertips. When she looked at him her eyes flooded with fresh tears.

"If we can be friends, at least I'll know we can be something more than nothing. I love you and I'm not afraid to admit it to anyone, but we can't be lovers anymore."

"I know," she sniffed. "It still doesn't stop the pain. If we can be friends, I'm pleased. I want you to know I will always be in love with you."

He smiled and she threw her arms around his neck. He held her tight as she rested her face against his shoulder.

They showered and dressed and ate breakfast. Cassidy toured him around the gallery and he admired all of her work. They walked hand in hand to have dinner by the fireplace and made love all night. Then she left him to sleep, careful not to disturb him. Mason was waiting for her when she arrived at home.

"Where's Roman? He should be home by now," she asked.

"He had to go to the gallery. A buyer is meeting him there. He was worried sick, but I assured him you were only out shopping. Where have you been, Cassie?" Mason interrogated.

"I wasn't far. I needed to sort some things out."

"Is that why your car was parked in Julian's garage?" He raised an eyebrow.

"If you knew, why didn't you tell him where I was?" she asked curiously as she hung up her coat.

"Because, I know you wouldn't do anything to jeopardize your marriage," Mason replied as he stood. He walked to her and put his hands on her shoulders. "I know that you needed to talk to him."

"We talked. Then we decided to be friends."

Mason sighed with relief.

"It was your influence that sent him away. Why?"

He looked away guiltily. "I thought it would be better if he let you go."

"How could you make a decision like that? Mason, you're my brother, not my father. Couldn't you see that he was in love with me?" Cassidy cried angrily.

"I didn't want to hurt you, Cassie. I felt like any minute he would turn on you. I didn't trust him," he defended.

"You were wrong about him." She turned away, trying to understand. "Don't play with my life, Mason. I will only end up hating you, and that's not what I want."

"All I can do is apologize. I was wrong, Cassie. Julian was in love with you," he admitted.

"It's too late to apologize. Maybe not to me, but to Julian. He's still in love with me, and he's still hurting," she pointed out.

"I'll talk to him."

"Promise?" she faced him.

"Yeah," he nodded. Cassidy smiled and hugged him. He kissed the top of her head.

CHAPTER TEN

Two months later Mason and Lacey were married. The wedding was beautiful. The reception was exciting and the two newlyweds were so happy and in love. Roman sat at the wedding party table. He had had his share of champagne and was gazing angrily at the dance floor. Cassidy smiled although her bulging middle made her seem less than cultivated, or light on her feet. Julian didn't seem to mind.

"Is it me or the champagne, Mason?" Roman asked.

"What?" Mason gave him his attention.

"The gentle way she looks at him, like she's his wife and not mine."

Mason looked out at his sister and best friend. It was clearly on their faces. Anyone would have thought that they were a couple. He smiled and turned back to Roman. "I think it's the champagne."

"Maybe," Roman shrugged.

Julian smiled, "You were the prettiest bridesmaid there."

"Well, I feel like a Thanksgiving turkey, all stuffed and roasting," she replied.

"I think you're beautiful," he stated.

After the song was over Mason and Julian went up to the bandstand. Cassidy sat down next to Roman who put his hand over hers and gave it a loving squeeze. Cassidy listened to her brother as he joked with Julian, until they decided to sing a song. A chair was brought to the center of the dance floor and Lacey's father escorted her to sit there. She was simply glowing. Her blonde hair hung in golden ringlets and her veil was fastened in place with pins that were hidden in baby's breath. She smiled longingly at her new husband.

"We'd like to dedicate this song to the women we love. Ladies, this is for you," Mason said before the music began.

Lacey smiled with a special bridal sparkle in her eyes. The room had dimmed so that the stage was brightly lit. When Cassidy focused on Julian she realized that he wasn't looking in Rachelle's direction, but in hers. Cassidy's heart ached to be able to gaze back at him so intently. Julian paused when she got up from the table and left the room. She stood in the night air and let the breeze dry her tears. She embraced herself not knowing exactly how to pull herself together when Julian's love was so clearly on his face.

After she caught her breath and opened hers eyes to look around someone came up behind her.

"Accept this rose and know that it symbolizes all that we had," echoed in her head, even though Julian didn't speak, he just held the white flower out for her to take. Cassidy turned around and met his eyes. His fingers caressed her cheeks and then her lips felt his brush passed them. She took the rose and hugged him tightly.

Julian squeezed his eyes closed and then brought her lips back to his. They met again and again until their kiss was deep and long, and fire was all around them, with burning desire. Mason spotted them, and when Cassidy saw him she pulled back and looked away. Mason pretended like he didn't see their kisses, stepping forward.

"Cassie, I think it's time you take Roman home. He's had a lot to drink. I'll get him out here and you pull the car around. OK?" he said.

"OK," she replied as he dropped the keys in her hand.

She watched Julian walk away from her with Mason. She found the car and got in. After starting it, she broke into tears and sat there crying into her hands, before she pulled around the front. Mason and Julian got Roman into the passenger seat and buckled him in. She rolled down her window as she gazed at Julian, he could see she laid the rose across the dashboard. Mason leaned in.

"Julian is going to follow you home. You won't be able to get Roman in the house in your condition."

"Mason?"

"Yeah?"

She straightened his white bow tie and kissed his cheek. "I'm so happy for you. Have a careful and safe trip. OK?" she said.

"We'll call you from the ship to let you know we're all right," he nodded.

"Thanks."

While Julian got Roman upstairs and into bed, Cassidy made some coffee. Roman was out like a light before his head hit the pillow. Julian came down and sat at the table. He loosened his tie and slipped it off and into his tuxedo jacket that he rested over the back of the chair. He smiled at Cassidy as she poured them each a cup of coffee.

"Are you hungry? I could heat something up real

quick," she suggested.

"No. I'm fine," he replied.

"OK." She sat down next to him.

It was silent for a long time. Cassidy laid her right hand on the table and tapped her fingernails. Julian was sipping from his cup when he realized she was still wearing his ring. Then he put his hand over hers and she spread her fingers so he could lace his with hers.

"You still wear this?" he pointed out.

"Actually, the only time I've ever taken it off was when Roman asked me to marry him. Even then I just put it on this hand. I get so many compliments on this ring for some reason." She smiled up at him. "It's my favorite, even though I have more flashier ones in my jewelry box." She shrugged and sipped from her cup. "Sometimes when I'm painting I look over and see it, and I can feel how you put your arms around me when you proposed. I married Roman because I care about him. But, I've never been able to love him as much as I love you."

"Cass," he smiled and touched her face, although his eyes were heartbroken. "I should go. I'll be busy while Mason is away." Julian stood and picked up his jacket.

Cassidy saw something that was in his eyes he was hiding from her. She stood as he ran his fingers through his hair. He turned and walked out of the room and headed for the front door. Cassidy followed him outside and caught his arm before he got into his car.

"Let me go, Cassidy."

"Talk to me. I can see something is bothering you," she said.

"I don't know if you'll understand."

"Tell me anyway."

He swallowed and looked up at the sky. Julian could smell the rain coming, and then he looked down at her. "I'm angry at Mason for marrying Lacey. It's not fair for him to be so happy while I am lying in my bed at night aching for you to be by my side. Maybe I'm jealous, but for some reason I'd love to see him hurting right now," his voice was tight. "He stole you away from me, because he didn't trust me."

He turned away from her and tried to put out his anger, when she slipped her arms around his waist. Julian held her there feeling a lump in his throat. He felt tears stinging the back of his eyes. Then he turned and rested his face in her fresh smelling hair.

"I understand you more than you know, Jule. I had the same feeling when he slipped the ring on her finger. All I could think about was you and I. When will we have our glory? He's my brother, Jule. I already forgave him."

Julian breathed and smiled as the rain began and then their tears were obsolete and their kisses took away their pain. "I love you, Cassidy. I need you."

She smoothed back his soaked hair and he opened the door for her to get in. He was so tender that night that Cassidy didn't want to go home. Julian waited for her to fall asleep and then carried her inside. He found a blanket and covered her after laying her on the sofa in the living room. Then he brushed the loose strands of hair away from her face, before he kissed her forehead and left out the door to quietly drive away.

Roman came downstairs holding his head. He was wearing a robe and longed for fresh coffee. The maid already had the breakfast table set and ready. He spotted his wife still asleep on the mauve sofa. He sat beside her and kissed her cheek. Cassidy reached out for him without opening her eyes.

"I love you, Julian," she whispered in his ear.

"What did you call me?" Roman got up and roared, startling her into reality.

"Oh God, Roman. I didn't mean it," she said quickly.

"You've been seeing him haven't you?" he shouted.

"Roman, I — " Cassidy was cut off and pulled to her feet. He made her look at him.

"Answer me, Cassidy!" He shook her.

"I'm so sorry, Roman. Please …"

Roman was so angry instantly, like he'd been waiting for her to tell him she was having an affair with Julian all this time. He let her go and she fell to the floor. She'd never seen him so angry as he went around the room breaking all of their beautiful things. All at once she became so frightened of him.

When the maid rushed out to see what was happening, Roman was shouting obscenities and then he suddenly stopped. He grabbed an old antique pistol from the mantle and snatched Cassidy to her feet.

"Listen to me carefully, Cassidy Spencer. If he ever touches you again, I'll kill him! Forget him, Cassidy. I swear I'll shoot him and I won't loose any sleep over it!" Roman finished and stormed upstairs.

Cassidy, still shaken and frightened, sat there dumbfounded. Then she darted to the closet and grabbed her purse and keys.

Roman heard the door slam and ran back down the

stairs. He rushed outside to chase her, but she screeched away. Everything had happened so fast that she was afraid to go home. She waited for the iron gates to open in front of her brother and Julian's estates. Then she drove in and parked in front of Mason's mansion. Richard, her brother's chauffer, pulled it into the garage.

"Mrs. Spencer, is something wrong, ma'am?" Hazel asked. Cassidy stared at the old woman for a moment.

"Who are you?" Cassidy asked.

"I'm your brother's new housekeeper, Mrs. Hazel Barnes. "Didn't he tell you?" she asked, in a distinct, heavy British accent.

Cassidy smiled. Hazel had the kindest gray eyes she had ever seen. "No, he didn't. It's nice to meet you, Hazel."

"Is there something I can get you?" she shook Cassidy's hand.

"No. I'm going to lie down for a while. If Mr. Spencer comes over or phones, I don't want to see or talk to him. OK?"

"Very well, Miss Cassidy," Hazel nodded and left the foyer.

Cassidy walked into her bedroom, and collapsed on the big bed. She was grateful for her brother saving this room for her, and fell into a dreamless sleep, trying to forget Roman's harsh anger. She awoke to feel someone stroking her messy hair softly and slowly. When she opened her eyes she gazed up into Julian's concerned expression. Gently she reached to touch his face before she let her hand fall back to her side.

"Jule," she breathed.

"Yeah, it's me. I saw Richard pull your car in the

garage. What's wrong?" he asked, cradling her in his arms.

"It's nothing really. I had a fight with Roman," Cassidy explained as she looked away and sat up.

Julian's hands dropped into his lap. He watched her get up and walk into the bathroom. He heard the water running in the sink and got up. He paced the room and ran his finger through his chestnut waves. When she came out she wouldn't look at him. Cassidy fumbled through the dresser and pulled out a shirt that wouldn't fit over her and her baby, and sighed. Julian disappeared down the hall and returned with one of her brother's long sleeved suit shirts.

"Tell me what Roman said, Cass."

"It was nothing, OK? I don't want to talk about it," she snapped, then starting brushing her hair.

Julian walked over to her and spun her around. Then he lifted her chin so she had to look at him. Cassidy tried to push him away, but he had already seen the tears she was trying to control. "Julian, stop it. Just go away. Please."

"Talk to me. I can't stand it. You used to tell me everything. Don't shut me out," he reminded.

"That was before you walked out on me," her words and voice were harsh.

She had to bite her tongue to keep from apologizing. She knew it would be better for him to hate her than to see Roman hurt him.

Julian straightened and flashed her his hurt look before he left, slamming the door behind him. It seemed like she had no other option, but to forget the only man she truly loved. Roman was a man of his word and she knew that.

Cassidy turned and leaned against the wall, slowly sliding to the floor where she began to sob into her hands.

Julian came back and knelt in front her, taking her hands in his. She pushed him away, standing.

"Julian get out! Leave me alone!" She pushed him again as hard as she could. "I hate you! You walk out of my life and then try to slip back in. It doesn't work that way. All I was to you was another heart to step on!" she accused.

"That's not true," he said in his defense. "I —"

"Don't, OK? Lies! That's all you've ever said to me. Now get out!" She faltered then, and put her hands over her face.

"What do I have to say to make you believe that I love you?" Julian asked.

"There's nothing you could say," she hissed, using the same words he had the day he left her.

Cassidy lay awake for hours watching television, only thinking about the last twenty-four hours. The look of bitterness and anger in Roman's eyes really frightened her. He'd always been a calm and rational man. Then again, he had every right to be upset and she knew it. A knocking at her door startled her back into reality.

"Cassidy, ma'am?" Hazel called.

"Yes?"

"I brought you a tray. You must be starved indeed," she replied.

"Oh, thank you, Hazel. My baby must be wondering …" she paused when she opened the door to find Roman holding a tray. Hazel stood behind him silently apologizing. Cassidy nodded to her and she left.

Cassidy closed the door and put her hands on her hips as she stared at her husband. He was casually dressed in jeans and a tee shirt, with running shoes. His dusty brown hair was gathered in a ponytail that hung short.

"Darling, please forgive me. I know I lost my temper, but I didn't mean it. I love you. I guess I'm jealous when it comes to you. Can you blame me? I feel so badly," he explained and walked over to her.

"I didn't mean for it to happen, Roman. It just did. This was my fault. I should be apologizing to you."

"No. It's my fault. If I hadn't insisted that Julian come to our anniversary party, to show you off like an idiot, none of this would have ever happened. I don't blame you, Cassidy."

She smiled at him softly and then slipped her arms around his neck and felt him hold her close. The baby kicked and Roman felt it and laughed. He reached down to caress his wife's swollen belly. "I think the baby wants in the picture, too."

"I think he would like some of that food you brought up," she smiled.

After Roman left ahead of her in his car, Richard had hers waiting for her outside. Before she got in, after thanking him, she caught sight of Julian standing out on the balcony. The bitter cool breeze blew his hair back as he looked back at her. Carefully she waved and he looked away. She wanted to run to him and be in the strength of his arms again, but she got into her car and sped off as fast as she could.

CHAPTER ELEVEN

When Lacey and Mason returned home from their honeymoon and settled in, Lacey threw Cassidy a huge surprise baby shower. Cassidy was overwhelmed with all of her friends and the gifts they'd brought for the baby. Mason had taken Roman to a ball game he'd been excited to see. Nothing had been the same between them, and the excitement of their baby was the only thing keeping them solid for the time. Cassidy gathered a plate full of cake and waddled through her brother's house.

She noticed when she passed the den that it was lit up with a dancing flame only a fire could make. When she peeked in curiously, Julian was sitting alone staring thoughtfully into the flames. He was smoking a cigarette and drinking from a cocktail glass. Cassidy sat down in the chair next to him and smiled. He drunkenly gazed her way, and swallowed what was left in his glass. He stood and inhaled the last of his cigarette before tossing it into the fire.

"Burning thoughts?" she asked.

"Trying to. Want … a drink?" He hiccupped and staggered to the bar to pour another glass of scotch.

"I'll have a soda, if you've got one," she replied.

"Enjoying your party?"

"It's all right. I'd rather sit with you where it's quiet for a while if you don't mind." She took another bite of cake.

"Really?" Julian raised an eyebrow as he stumbled back to the chair almost spilling the drinks. "I thought you — hated me."

"Julian, I was upset when I said that. I had a fight with Roman and he said some things, and I was ... I was upset. I knew he'd come here looking for me, so I said what I did so he wouldn't find us together. I'm sorry. I was only protecting you from a vicious conflict," she explained.

"I can take care of ... myself. Thank you."

"Fine. I'm sorry I bothered you," Cassidy finished and stood to leave.

Julian clumsily beat her to the door and locked it behind him. He stood there trying to collect his intoxicated senses. Cassidy looked down. "I'm sorry, Cass. Stay with ... me for — a while. Please?"

"I miss you so much, Jule. I can't sleep or do anything without thinking about you. Last night I was painting and ended up painting you. Roman watches every move I make." Tears flooded her eyes as she touched his face. "I'd do anything to be with you, even if we can't be lovers anymore. I just want to be with you. Talk to you."

"Let me hold you, Cass. I need to hhhold you close ... for a minute."

Cassidy set her plate down and fell against him as his arms encircled her. She rested her face in the hollow of his neck. Julian could feel her warm tears as they began to flow. The smell of her perfume drove him mad with the desire to make love to her so freely, like he'd once been able to do. The feelings he had wouldn't go away, and they weren't even numbed by the sting of the scotch. No other woman had ever made him feel this way.

He lifted her chin to his and dried the wet paths with his thumbs. Cassidy put her hands on his face and pressed her lips to his again and again until she felt his lips part and they were kissing long and deeply. They kissed until they couldn't breathe and clung to each other gasping for air.

"I have to go before Lacey comes looking for me. I love you, Jule. I love you more than I can say," she whispered into his ear before she disappeared through the double doors.

Julian squeezed his eyes closed and lit a cigarette and inhaled deeply. Then he sat and put his face in his hands. Her perfume, on his palms and shirt, still lingered enticingly. Roman burst into the room and Julian looked up. Roman looked around and then stared at him as he inhaled from his cigarette, never letting his eyes away from Roman's for a second. Roman looked down.

"Would you like a drink?" Julian asked after standing and swallowing his completely.

"No. Thank you," he replied.

"Cigarette?" Julian smiled offering him one.

"No."

"There you are, Roman," Lacey said, coming into the room. "Cassidy needs to go home. She's not feeling well."

"Is she all right?" both men asked at the same time.

"Well … I think she's just had enough excitement for one day."

"All right," Roman replied. Lacey stayed behind to talk to Julian.

When she turned to look at him, his expression was sad, after only seconds he was ready to go to war. He crushed out his cigarette. Lacey caught hold of his arm, but didn't hang on. He looked at her kindly for steadying him and smiled.

"Cassidy's OK, right?" he asked. "I don't think I could stand it if anything ever happened to her."

"She's fine, Julian. She just needs a lot of rest," Lacey assured.

"Where's Mason?"

"Probably attacking what's left on the buffet," she smiled.

"Sounds like a good idea to me," he sighed and left the room to join his friend.

The fresh canvas leaned blank on Cassidy's easel. She held her brush as she gazed at it vacantly. Her thoughts were clouded, and suddenly for the life of her, she couldn't understand why she had come to paint at all. With a sigh she put everything away and went to her brother's studio. He was alone practicing a ballad when she sat quietly to listen.

Julian came out of his office. He was dressed in jeans and a turquoise tee shirt. It seemed strange to see him so casually dressed. He'd always been so carefully elegant with his wardrobe. When he noticed her sitting with a smile on her face he gave her a polite nod. Mason turned and smiled.

"I didn't hear you come in, Cassie," Mason said.

"I didn't want to disturb you. Whatever you were singing was lovely," she replied, standing as quickly as her bulging middle would let her.

"I'm starving. What do you two say about having a lunch trio?" Mason rubbed his hands together, glancing from his sister to his friend.

"I'm up for it," Cassidy said. "How about you, Julian?"

"Sure. Why not?" he smiled.

Julian had to laugh at the sight of Cassidy's face when the waitress brought out the ice cream sundae she had ordered. "Oh, come on. One of you can help me eat this. I'm supposed to gain a little weight, but I'm not that desperate.

"Well, I have to go pick up Lacey from the hospital. So have fun," Mason teased as he got up.

"Pay backs are hell, Mason," Cassidy scoffed before he was out of earshot.

Julian picked up his spoon. "I hope this child of yours appreciates this."

"Not as much as I do, Jule." She breathed with relief.

After they finished, they walked through the park and sat on the swings to talk. When Julian lit a cigarette, Cassidy glared at him with disappointment. He laughed and offered her one. She shook her head even though she was tempted.

"I can't. I've been real good about quitting, too. After the baby is born you can bring me my first one."

"It's a deal," he nodded.

"God, it's gorgeous out here. I love spring."

"Yes. I remember," he replied.

"What are we doing together, Julian? Roman has a terrible temper concerning you now. He threatened to kill you if he found out you were with me again."

"Is that what that was all about three months ago? That little scene after Mason's wedding?"

"Pretty much. I could never let anyone hurt you, Julian. Not when I can save you," Cassidy stated.

She got up from the swing beside him and folded her arms. "It was just an argument. It was my fault. I don't really want to talk about it." She pivoted back to him. "If I can find a way out of this marriage, I will. I wanted you to know that. Because I want to be with you."

Julian nodded and stood with understanding before he kissed her softly and they walked back to the car holding hands.

CHAPTER TWELVE

When Cassidy walked in the door, dinner was waiting for her. Roman was sitting at his end of the table sipping from a glass of wine. She washed her hands and then joined him. He was very quiet as they ate. Cassidy looked over at him curiously. "Is there something wrong?" she asked.

"Where were you today?" Roman snapped.

"I was with Mason. I couldn't concentrate on painting so I went over to spend the day with him. We had lunch in the plaza," Cassidy replied.

"I saw you, Cassidy. I saw you with him today."

"With Mason?"

"No!" he roared and knocked his plate to the floor. "I saw you with Julian."

"He had lunch with us," she replied.

"I didn't see your brother with you at the park when I drove by. I saw you sitting on the swings with Julian."

"Listen. We were just talking — " she was cut off.

Roman stood and tossed the painting of Julian on the table. Then he slammed his fist down on it startling her. "It's very good, darling. It should be a good portrait to display over his casket!"

"Roman, please. I can't just cut him off as a friend even, I care about him," she exclaimed.

"Oh yes, you can. And, believe me you will," he finished.

Cassidy stood up and went after him. "This isn't fair, Roman."

He spun around fast. "It isn't fair? You know Julian used to be one of my best friends. It was he, Mason, George Davenport and I. We all went to college together. We all played poker and ran off to Las Vegas one time. We were crazy and we loved it. But, everyone grew up, Cassidy. This isn't like it used to be when we would all try out the same girl. You are my wife! That's where it ends."

"I believe that, too. But, you can't take away how I feel. You can't change it," she insisted.

"We'll see," Roman nodded and walked away slamming his den door.

Nothing was right between them since that night. Cassidy knew it was only a matter of time before he lost his temper completely. But, he held it in and did his best to make things right. He finished the murals in the nursery and set up the furniture to surprise her. Every night he came in with a half gallon of her favorite ice cream and rubbed her shoulders to put her to sleep. When he thought she was asleep he would slip his hand beneath her nightgown to feel his unborn child move.

Cassidy hardly had the energy to move anymore. She couldn't even fit behind the steering wheel of her car to go anywhere. It had been weeks since she had heard from Lacey and Mason. They were both so involved in their separate work. Cassidy swallowed her pain and hadn't seen or spoken to Julian in over a month. She had received a letter, but she hid it away in drawer without reading it.

Julian sat in his office cleaning out his desk, when he ran across an old picture. A picture of him with Cassidy right after they first met. They were so happy then, so completely in love right from the start. It tore him up inside, and now not being able to see her was hurting more than a knife twisting in his side. He looked up then and Cassidy was standing in the doorway.

"I was just thinking about you. How did you get here?" Julian asked jumping to his feet to help her in and hold her out a chair to sit.

"I took a cab. I came to see Mason. Where is he?" she asked.

"He left about ten minutes ago to get us some lunch. He should be back soon," he smiled. "I haven't seen you lately. How are you?"

"Fine. Ready to have this baby," she joked.

"I think I'd be uncomfortable, too," Julian agreed.

Cassidy saw the picture in his hand and gazed at it curiously. Tears filled her eyes and she looked away. Julian tossed it back into his drawer, and then stood to kneel in front of her. He dried her cheeks with his handkerchief and lifted her chin to look at her.

"It will be OK. We will get over it. I know you are hurting," he said with tenderness.

"You are, too. I could see it in your eyes when I came in. I want to forget all this pain, but how can I, Julian? I'm so in love with you," Cassidy cried. "Roman means nothing to me now. I can't even look at him anymore. All we do is fight. He is trying hard, but it's not fair to him. It's not fair to us! I wish I were dead!"

"Don't say that, Cass," he said, putting his arms around her. "I'll go away again. I can't stand to see you this way. If I leave, you can learn to forget about me again."

"I'll never forget you, Julian. Don't you leave me. Maybe I can't always see you or talk to you, but not to see you at all would crush me. Just hold me. Hold me tight. I need to feel your strength if only for a few minutes," Cassidy sniffed.

In his arms she buried her face in his shoulder in desperation, and he kissed her head. Trembling she touched his face and covered his mouth with hers. Their kisses were long and forbidden and they knew it. Suddenly they sank into the softness of the carpet. Cassidy unbuttoned his shirt and pushed it away from his chest. Her hands ran down over his stomach and up his back, then paused at the brim of his waist.

Julian touched her swollen belly and kissed her cheek, before he slid her dress casually up the side of her leg. Cassidy caught his arm then and met his eyes. Tears were swelling at the edges, fighting to fall.

"I want you. I want you now, here on the floor. I don't even care if I burn in hell, as long as I can be a part of you right now. I'll treasure every touch, every caress, every kiss you give, even if it's the last time we'll ever embrace," Julian breathed. "I love you."

"Even with another man's child inside of me?" Cassidy asked breathlessly.

"Yes."

She kissed him long and hard. Then they made love on the floor of Julian's office without hesitation or guilt. It made their bond stronger when they shared that tender place they knew only too well. Cassidy moved away and stood with his help as she went into the bathroom to dress. Julian put on his pants and had his shirt halfway buttoned when Mason burst in with a bag.

"I came to apologize for being late with your lunch. I guess you had a nap," he smiled and walked past him, to pause when he saw his sister come from the bathroom.

Even Cassidy stopped short when she saw her brother while she was fumbling with an earring. Her hands dropped to her sides. She had to look away from him. Mason ran his hand through his hair as he looked from his friend to his sister. Cassidy looked at Julian ashamed. He could see her tears glistening.

"You have to stop, Cassie. Don't throw your marriage away like it's nothing. Roman has given you five years of his devotion. He loves you. Why are you doing this?" Mason asked.

"I don't love him, Mason. If you weren't so blind you'd realize it," she replied.

"This is my fault. I shouldn't have come back," Julian stepped in. "But how can you take his side so easily? How can you look at us and not see the love we share? How can you look at us, Mason, and not see how we are hurting?"

"You should stay the hell away from my sister! I didn't want you around her in the first place!" Mason's anger burst.

Julian laughed, "I'm the one who brought her back to you. Maybe I should have just kept her for myself," he shot back.

Cassidy wedged herself between the two men. "Stop it! Please," she cried. "I can't take this. I can't take seeing you fight. Don't make me choose between you, Mason."

"Don't you threaten me, Cassidy Spencer," Mason said, pointing a finger. "I've known Roman a long time — "

"You don't know Roman! You don't know him at all!" she shouted and then fell forward with a moan.

Mason moved to catch her. "What is it, Cassie?"

"My water just broke. I'm … in labor," she sobbed, feeling a spear of lightening across her middle. "Oh God!"

Julian swung her up in his arms and rushed her out to his car. Mason called Roman and Lacey from his car phone as he reached back to hold his sister's hand as she panted in the backseat.

A nurse met them at the counter with a wheelchair. Cassidy kicked it away and began to walk down the hallway while holding onto the wall. Mason was suddenly thrown an outfit to put on over his clothes and shoved into the delivery room, while Julian waited in the hallway.

"Mason," Cassidy grabbed him by his shirt and pulled him to her. "I can't do this."

"Cassie, you have to, darling. You have to," he returned.

Everything that was happening was only a blur. She was filled with a combination of excitement, exhaustion, pain and fear. She tried to remember all of her Lamaze courses, but the distress made it difficult for her to concentrate. Once one contraction ended another began. Mason couldn't understand how he even got there, but did what the nurses suggested.

"All right!" Cassidy gasped. "I gotta push. Mason, I gotta push. Help me, God. Where's my husband?"

"He'll be here, Cassie. Breathe. Just breathe, sweetie," Mason said, and switched hands when he felt her squeeze the hell out of the other.

"Get it out!" she cried.

"OK, Cassidy, push," the doctor said, and she bared down as hard as she could with her contraction, and then fell back to catch her breath as tears and sweat poured down her face.

When Mason saw what was happening he felt flushed, but couldn't take his eyes away for a second in amazement. He began to laugh and cry at the same time when he saw his precious and pink screaming niece push her way into the world. "Cassie, you did it. You did it, honey! There she is."

Cassidy panting sat slightly with Mason's help, to look upon her infant daughter for the first time and carefully reached for her with an overcome grin. "She's so beautiful."

Roman rushed in out of breath and went to his wife like a magnet. He kissed her several times until a nurse handed him their daughter wrapped in a soft white blanket. His face fell not knowing what emotion to feel, and his eyes flooded with tears. Mason went out into the hallway to his wife and Julian. They both turned impatiently.

"It's a girl," he bubbled, and they all embraced happily.

When Roman took his daughter clumsily into his arms, he smiled tenderly and ran his finger over her soft tiny cheek. "My mother named me and my sisters after the last person she was alone with before going into labor. I was named after my father."

"We couldn't do that." She looked away.

"Why?"

"I went to see Mason, and he wasn't there. I was waiting for him. I was with Julian," she said softly.

Roman gave her a bruised look. Then he went out of the

room with the baby. In the hall he strode and paused in front of his brother-in-law, who took her carefully. Roman moved in front of Julian and looked him straight in the eye. "Her name is Julianna, after the last person Cassidy was alone with before she went into labor."

"Roman, I — " Julian was cut off.

"Tell me you haven't been having an affair again. I want to hear it from you, Drake!" he shouted angrily.

"I can't tell you that," he replied. "Because we never had one in the first place. Not like you think."

Mason took the baby back into the room and handed her to the nurse. Roman fell into the nearest chair. The shock in his eyes then turned to fire, and he lunged at Julian. Mason held them back, as an orderly came to help. Julian turned and was escorted out of the hospital. Lacey stood there with her hands on her face in tears. She had no idea what was going on. Everyone was so happy and then angry. When Roman caught himself and calmed, he went back in to his wife.

"Cassidy, he seduced you, right? Julian talked you into his bed, didn't he?"

"I am in love with him, Roman. I can't deny it. Julian didn't make me do anything I didn't want to," she admitted regretfully.

"What about us? What about the baby?" he asked.

"Let me go, Roman. I've been trying to tell you, but you won't listen. I don't love you, Roman."

"No. I won't let you go. I'll never let you go to that son of a bitch without a fight. Never!" he spat.

CHAPTER THIRTEEN

Julianna had her mother's face and her father's hair color. She was a happy baby and everyone fussed over her constantly. When she was five or six months old Cassidy began painting again, while Lacey and Mason would take turns with their niece. Julian felt Julianna playing with his shoelaces. He gazed around the room, and then leaned over to see her smiling up at him. She was learning to crawl and every chance she got she loved to make Julian her favorite playmate.

"What are you doing down there, little one?" he asked. "I bet your Aunt Lacey is looking all over for you."

Julian smiled and patted his shoes. "I think that I should warn you that your Uncle Mason has just invested in a playpen for you, young lady."

Lacey stood in the doorway silently watching them. Julian carefully lifted Julianna in his arms, and played with her softly, as a father would. Then he cradled her in the crook of his arm, and talked to her gently. Julianna was completely infatuated by him and his voice and wanted nothing more than to be close to him whenever she could. Julian would never admit melting to her charms.

"Maybe Uncle Julian wouldn't mind giving Julie her bottle?" Lacey suggested, holding it out for him to take as he shifted.

"Not me. No way. I was just going to bring the little

insect to you," he replied, changing his attitude for public appearance.

Lacey grinned and took the baby in her arms. "She'll be disappointed."

"Sorry. When is her mother coming to get her anyway?"

"Soon. Why?" Lacey tried not to laugh even as the child reached out for him as she squirmed.

"The sooner the better. Maybe then Mason and I can get some work done," Julian said grumpily.

"I see. Well … I have a photo of the little insect for your wallet. I'll set it on the table. Take it or leave it. It doesn't matter. Oh, and Mason is in by the piano waiting for you."

"All right."

Julian waited for Lacey to leave the room, before he stood and started past the table. He paused and backed up to pick up the picture, but wanted to make sure no one was looking. He quickly put it in his wallet, before going out to meet Mason.

Cassidy came in to plop in the first seat she could fine when she came to pick up her daughter. She was drinking from a bottle of water and her amber hair was tied in a tangled ponytail. Lacey sat down across from her and they began talking. Julianna scooted away from them.

"I think I've had enough of aerobic exercise. Besides, if I wanted buns of steel, I'd never have gotten pregnant in the first place," Cassidy remarked.

"I don't know why you're doing it anyway. You look great," Lacey said.

"I guess I do it to get away for an hour. Roman and I have settled into a daily routine of as soon as the baby's in bed we argue downstairs, so she can't hear us," Cassidy sighed. "He will have to give in sooner or later won't he?"

"I think he's holding on because he thinks you'll take Julie away from him," Lacey replied, and they walked into the kitchen as they looked for the baby.

"Lacey, I couldn't do that. How could I? They adore each other so much."

"I think Julie has a boyfriend you should know about. Every time I look away for a second she's off looking for Julian," she laughed. "The funny thing is, she knows exactly where to look for him. He acts like she's a pest, but when no one's around he loves her to pieces."

Cassidy gave her a strange look and followed her sister-in-law into where Mason and Julian were. Quietly they peeked in to see Julianna at Julian's feet tugging at his pant leg. Cassidy had to cover her mouth so she wouldn't laugh. When Mason wasn't looking Julian would smile softly, but then continue his singing. Lacey closed the door and they moved away so they wouldn't hear them.

"Isn't that something? And, Mason pretends like he doesn't see, but he does," Lacey pointed out.

"It is so sweet," Cassidy agreed before they went in to get the child.

Mason turned to them. "Cassie, you're back."

"I told you I'd only be gone an hour," she returned.

Julian hadn't seen her since Julianna was born. Even though she was dressed in exercise clothes and no make-up, she looked beautiful. "You don't need to lose weight. You look wonderful."

"All I'm doing is toning a bit. But, thanks, Jule," Cassidy smiled with a blush.

"Julie came in for some piano lessons," Mason laughed, as she banged on the keys from his lap.

"Well, then she came to the right place, didn't she?" Lacey put in.

Cassidy moved to pick her daughter up and kissed her cheeks and then her chubby belly giving it a blow. Julianna laughed and wrapped her arms around her mother's face to press her mouth against her cheek. It was a clumsy kiss, but Cassidy loved it and hugged her tight. "Miss me, did you, darling?"

"Why don't you stay for dinner, Cassie?" Mason suggested.

"No. I should go. The last thing I need is another argument. I try to avoid them as much as I can. Besides, Roman hasn't seen her all day," she replied.

"How about a drink later in the week?" Julian questioned to see her reaction.

"I'd love to, Julian. You let me know when you become invisible so Roman won't see you, and I'll meet you at the pub. No problem," she said with sarcasm. Mason looked down and Lacey was silent. "Listen. There isn't anything I want more right now than a divorce. Maybe one day my dear brother will admit that I'm not happy, and take pity on me. I can't divorce him so easily, without a lawyer that knows how to deal with this man's excessive temper. You both went to college with him, I wish one of you would have warned me."

"Cassie, I — " Mason was cut off.

"I do care about him, but sooner or later I'm going to end up hating him for the wrong reasons. He's miserable and so am I. It isn't a secret anymore."

"I was at the gallery the other day, Cassidy. You two seemed happy enough to me," Lacey replied.

"We're both wonderful actors, aren't we? The gallery is important to both of us. Business is good. If we begin to let our private life slip in front our business, we'll lose it," she explained.

"Cass … " Julian touched her shoulder.

"Don't, Jule. You and Mason can't afford to lose your partnership, either. I'm not worth it," she finished with bitterness and left.

Mason looked away, but Julian went after her and caught her after she strapped Julianna into her car seat. She paused with control and he pulled her into his arms. Cassidy clung to him briefly before she moved back and kissed his cheek. She sat in her car and rolled down the window to squeeze his fingers reassuringly before she pulled away and drove out of the estate. He could have kicked himself, but instead continued to walk home.

Lacey folded the bedspread down neatly and crawled into bed angrily. Mason got in next to her and went to kiss her but she turned cold on him and turned away. He sat up and sighed as he ran his fingers through his blond curls. Then he folded his hands beneath his chin. "What do you want me to do, Lacey?"

"Not a damn thing," she replied flatly.

"Come on," he moaned, and got out of bed to pace the floor.

"Help her. Roman is a different person to her than he is with us. I like him, too, but if his temper is that short how can you trust him? Julian is your best friend. He hasn't had a new relationship in years. For appearances he calls

Rachelle Winters and she is a nice woman, but he doesn't care about her as anything but a friend."

"You didn't know Julian before, Lacey," Mason put in.

"So what. I remember the papers. I remember his reputation, but when he met your sister he changed. She turned him into a man. Before he was still a college student that was a rising star living it up to conquer as many women as he could. How hard is it for you to see that? Julian is completely in love with her. If he was foolish enough to believe in your advice when you were just being selfish, he'd do anything for her. You're like his brother, Mason. Imagine how you hurt him, when you married me after telling him that you could never truly have a good marriage with your career. If I were Julian I'd have told you to go to hell a long time ago," she finished matter-of-factly and switched off the light.

Mason knew she was right. He had been unfair to his friend all these years. He deserved to be shunned. It was only that Cassidy was so extremely important to him, and he was afraid of Julian's childishness in the years behind. He knew that deep down Julian would hurt her. He crawled into bed and kissed his wife on the cheek before he lay awake to think about it.

CHAPTER FOURTEEN

Cassidy found herself going over the accounts with her accountant when Roman was out of town at another seminar. Her mind was only on Julian, as she let whatever James was saying go in one ear and out the other. Her daughter crawled across the floor to the television and clapped her hands as she giggled to Mason and Julian's new music video. She called her mother and slapped at the screen whenever Julian would appear. James finished and collected all his receipts before he left tickling the child under the chin.

"Julianna, do you know something Momma hasn't been telling you verbally?" she asked and the baby laughed. "You really shouldn't tempt me. Daddy doesn't like Uncle Julian."

Julianna's little face crumpled as she continued to beat the glass screen. Her little blue eyes flooded with tears, as her bottom lip started to quiver. Cassidy picked her up and Julianna sniffed against her mother's shoulder. "Who could resist a face like yours, Julie? Is it worth getting into another fight? Only if we get caught, right? Right," Cassidy replied, and went to freshen up.

Julian came out from under the race car to focus on mother and daughter. He was covered with dirt and grease as he stood up trying to wipe his hands on his grease rag. He smiled at Cassidy and then looked around to wave at his mechanics as they went inside. He went in the bathroom to scrub his hands clean and take off the overalls that protected his clothes.

"How about that drink, stranger?" Cassidy suggested.

"So where do you think we can find a bottle of milk with a couple of good glasses of wine?" he grinned.

"Actually, I thought maybe Aunt Lacey could mind her while we were out."

"Sounds like an idea to me. I need a shower anyway," he replied.

"What for? I love a rugged man with dirt in his hair, and sweat on his skin," Cassidy teased. "Maybe we can find another leather jacket like mine for you, and ride a motorcycle through the countryside. I didn't get all dressed up for nothing."

Julian laughed. Cassidy was wearing a black tank top tucked into her black jeans, with leather boots that came half way to her knees and a worn in leather jacket. Her amber hair was wild and her make-up down to perfection.

"Where do we get a motorcycle?"

"A dealership, of course."

In an hour Cassidy found herself riding with her arms around Julian's waist and her face pressed against the leather of his jacket. He smiled and felt her hand reach inside his shirt to caress his warm skin. He pulled off the road and parked to turn to her and covered her mouth with his. They threw off their helmets and ran behind a huge oak tree. As Cassidy leaned against the old tree she tried to catch her breath as Julian moved into her and touched her breasts through her thin top.

She ran her fingers through his shoulder length hair and

found his mouth as they passionately made love under the tree. Julianna was almost eight months old, and Roman hadn't made any attempt to touch her and she knew he was seeing other women. So when she climaxed in the middle of nowhere she called Julian's name over and over in her pleasure.

After they dressed she wrapped her legs around him as he carried her back to the motorcycle while they continued to kiss. Julian smiled as she helped him fasten his helmet back on and then they sped off back down the road.

Lacey decided to keep Julianna when Cassidy and Julian returned full of laughter after spending a wonderful afternoon making love and drinking tequila at the pub. They had a quiet dinner for two in the living room while watching a movie and holding each other, and then she knew she had to go, and stood to check her hair in the mirror before donning on her jacket. Julian came up behind her and slipped his arms around her waist to lean and kiss her cheek. Cassidy smiled at his reflection. Then she turned to face him.

"I can't remember when I have been so breath taken, Jule. I don't want to go," she said against his chin.

"Then stay," he replied.

"That is an argument I can do without. But thanks for the invitation. I love you."

"I love you, too," Julian finished and kissed her before she left.

When Cassidy came in the door, she was snatched up and thrown to the floor. Roman had beaten her home, hiding his car on the side of the house. He was in another rage, and she tried to stand before he grasped a handful of her hair and picked her up. He clenched her arms tightly and shook her until she was lightheaded. She screamed when he struck her across the cheek and pushed her again to the floor. Blood seeped through the cut his ring had made.

"You were with him again, weren't you?" he shouted.

"Yes! I was," she cried back. "And, you can beat me again and again, and tomorrow I'll go back to him, Roman. Let me go!"

"Never! He's a dead man, Cassidy! A dead man! Do you hear me?"

"Yes!" she cried out from the pressure he squeezed on her arm. She thought he'd snap it in two.

Roman left her there and slammed the door behind him. Slowly she stood and tried to collect herself as she made it out to her car. Then Cassidy fumbled with the phone, trying to find Mason, when he finally answered. He heard panic through her tears, but he couldn't make out what she was saying.

"Cassie, slow down. I can't understand a word you're saying."

"Roman's gonna kill him, Mason. Please don't let him through the gate," she cried.

"What?"

"Close the goddamned gate!" Cassidy yelled and slammed the phone down before he could say another word.

She pulled up behind her husband's car and barely put it in park before she hopped out. He turned to her angrily as she pleaded with him to come home with her. Mason and Lacey ran out of the house. Lacey was holding the baby close. She could see Cassidy and Roman, but she couldn't hear what they were saying.

Julian came out seeing Roman shaking Cassidy viciously. He stormed passed Mason and into Roman's view. "Julian, wait!"

Mason was too late. Julian had ordered the gate open and was at Roman's throat. He'd thrown him onto to his car and wouldn't let him up.

"Julian, let him go!" Mason shouted.

"Back off, Mason. You're so damned busy worrying about what I'm going to do to hurt your sister, that you're blind to what he's done to her," Julian said through his clenched teeth.

Cassidy thought he'd choke Roman to death and rushed to calm him. "Jule, please. He's not worth it. Please let him go."

"He hurt you, and I can't let that happen again," he replied. "You're not so bad now are you, Spencer? Does it make you feel better to beat up on a woman? Looks like I'm a bigger match for you."

"Go — to hell ... Drake," Roman struggled to say.

"Julian, please," Cassidy pleaded.

"Come on, Jule. Don't make me force the guards on you. Let him go," Mason said calmly.

"You hit her again, it'll be your undoing, you son of a bitch," he said before he released him.

Roman fell to the ground gasping for air. He coughed as Cassidy knelt by him in tears. She looked up at Julian angrily with blood and tears dripping off her chin. "You could have killed him!"

"Better for him to kill you then, right? You stay with

your precious husband, Cassidy. I don't want any part of it," Julian replied, hurt by her ease to snap at him. He started away but paused and turned his back to her. "Believe me, if I wanted him dead, he'd be dead."

Julian stormed passed Mason through the gate pausing only to take Julianna, so Lacey could check on Roman and Cassidy. She knelt next to Cassidy as soon as Mason got Roman into his car. Cassidy winced when her brother barely touched her face.

"Did he do this to you, Cassie?" Mason asked.

"It's nothing, Mason. Really." She looked away.

"Nothing? It's a lot to me. Stay with us. I'll get you that divorce, I swear I will. I can't have him hurting you or Julianna."

"Just take care of her for me. I have no choice but to deal with this, Julian doesn't understand. I'll be back for the baby later. My keys are in the ignition," she finished, looking Julian's way.

He wouldn't look at her. She felt more tears and drove her husband home.

Late that evening Mason wandered into Julian's den. He sat in the chair beside him, and lit a cigarette. They both sat in silence for a long time as they stared into the fire. Julian's anger in protecting Cassidy snapped Mason into reality. Especially the difference between him and Roman.

"I owe you an apology, my old friend. I was wrong about you. I was wrong in sending you away, and wrong in believing Roman could make Cassidy happy enough to forget you."

"You never even gave me a chance," Julian replied.

"I know. I am sorry."

"Apology accepted then," Julian smiled, and poured what was left in his whiskey bottle into the glass he held before he handed it to his partner.

"Cheers?" Mason offered.

"Cheers."

Cassidy lay in bed with her back to her husband. She couldn't sleep. Roman touched the back of hair and moved closer to her. She turned to look at him. He gently touched her bruised and cut cheek and looked down, ashamed. In the silvery moonlight of their bedroom he looked again upon her.

"I never meant to do this. I'm so sorry. It's just that we used to be so happy. Didn't you mean it when you married me? Didn't you love me?" he asked seriously.

"Roman, you made me forget for a little while. You moved in too soon and tried to take his place. Mason pushed it and I know he meant well, but it was wrong. Even if Julian hadn't come back, it wouldn't have worked." She sat up and sighed, "Sooner or later I'd have wanted out."

He got up out of bed and ran his hands through his hair. He sighed and took a deep breath before he started breaking things in a rampage. Cassidy moved back as he took his anger out on something rather than her. After he calmed down, Roman sat beside her again. He took her hands in his and held them tightly.

"Tell me you loved me, Cassidy. You did love me, didn't you?"

"I loved you, but not like I love Julian," she admitted. "I want a divorce, Roman. I've been asking you for months. Please?"

He kept shaking his head. "No. I can't. You'll take Julianna away from me, too, and what will I have? Forget it. I won't let you do it."

"I would never keep you from your daughter. I promise you that. Just let me go," she begged.

"I said it won't happen!" he snapped.

"Then I guess we'll be two very unhappy people," she finished and walked out.

Roman grabbed her by the arm and paused when she looked right through him. "Go ahead. Just remember who knows about your abuse. I'm sure it doesn't take much to remember how his fingers felt as they tightened around your neck."

Roman released her as he brought his fingers to his throat and swallowed. He stood there staring after her until she disappeared into the guestroom and slammed the door. There she crawled into bed and sobbed into her pillows until she finally found sleep.

Roman hadn't threatened her again after that night. He worked with her silently and at the gallery they continued to be happy for business purposes. Twice he'd come to her and had his way, but never left another mark. It was clear to her that Julian frightened him. It had been months since the incident, but she hadn't seen Julian since then.

Julianna had just had her first birthday and Lacey was helping Cassidy clean up. They were in the kitchen when the phone rang. "Lacey, would you? My hands are all soapy."

"Sure. Hello?"

"Mrs. Spencer?

"Yes. This is she," Lacey laughed after putting her hand over the bottom of the receiver. Cassidy smiled over at her.

"The results of your pregnancy test came in positive. Congratulations," the receptionist replied happily.

"Thank you."

"I've an opening for an appointment on Wednesday. Will that be all right?"

"Two o'clock? OK," Lacey said, checking Cassidy's appointment calendar. "I'll see you then."

"What was that all about?" Cassidy asked.

"Roman raped you, didn't he Cassie?" Lacey asked seriously.

Cassidy frowned and looked down into the sink. "I'm pregnant again?"

Her sister-in-law nodded.

"Actually, if I don't move he gets it over with and leaves me alone." She half smiled. "I think about Julian, and then take a hot shower. I guess it just wasn't enough. Oh, well."

Lacey watched as Cassidy tried to forget and finish what she was doing, but her face crumpled and she broke down and dropped a glass to shatter at her feet. Lacey embraced her. Mason brought in the last of the food, and paused to see the two women in tears. After Lacey told him what happened he pulled his sister into his arms and she clung to him tightly.

"I want out, Mason," she sniffed. "He won't let me go. I want to be with Julian."

"Leave him now. I'll finish here, and Lacey will help you pack. I can't stand to let him hurt you anymore,

Cassie. Come with us," he said.

"I need to be alone. I'm going for a drive. I need some air."

"Come on and pack, and we'll go for a drive. I'll go with you," Lacey suggested.

Cassidy ran to her car and pulled out of the driveway like a bat out of hell. She wanted to scream. She wanted to die, and yet now another life was inside her. She didn't know where she was going, even as tears kept flooding her eyes, and her throat ached to cry out, but she kept on driving. When she pulled in through the gate it was dark. Only one light glowed from the balcony and she knew he was there.

Cassidy fumbled to light a cigarette and her bottle slipped from her hand to shatter on the pavement. She stumbled to the door and went in, with the key that was hidden in the flowerpot. She didn't even wake the maid as she slipped off her shoes in the foyer and tried not to fall as she went up the stairs. Julian was asleep on his bed. He'd been reading and fell asleep before shutting off the lamp. Quietly she crushed out her cigarette and sat in the chair by him.

Julian was so beautiful to her. Cassidy folded her arms and then leaned to fold her hands beneath her chin as she shifted and rested her elbows on her knees.

She only wanted to be near him for a while. Julian brought her comfort even when he didn't know it. Her head was spinning as she closed her eyes, and her stomach churned from too much alcohol. Julian stirred then and her head snapped up. His eyes opened and he tried to focus. Then he reached blindly to shut off the light.

When he sighed and looked around, he saw her in the dark. He sat up and rubbed his eyes to make sure he wasn't dreaming. "Cassidy?"

"Yes?" she whispered back.

"He hurt you again, didn't he?"

"Jule?" She began to cry. "I hurt you. I — I never — meant to hurt you. I desperately need you in my … life. Roman's torturing me. Everyday … every second I cccan't be with you, is tearing me apart."

Julian reached for her then and pulled her into his arms. "Then stay with me."

"For how long, darling? Until dawn when reality hits, and closes us in?"

"It's all we've had for two years, Cass," he replied.

"I have to go. It's late," she said, although she still clung to him as if her words had no real meaning.

"Stay a little longer, it's been so long since I've held you." His lips curved upward in the moonlight.

Cassidy pulled away and sat up. She could feel the tears swelling in her eyes. His hand was combing through her hair and making her crazy. Julian knew something was wrong and was waiting for her to tell him what it was, but she couldn't. How could she tell him that she was pregnant with another one of Roman's children? She wanted it to be Julian's.

When she stood the room spun, but she made it to the door. Suddenly it closed and all she felt was the hardness of his male body. All she could feel was the warmth of his breath on the back of her neck. Her tears fell slowly sliding down her cheeks and dripped off her chin, his arms went around her pulling her close again.

"Don't go back to him," Julian whispered. "Stay with me. Let me make you happy again. Let me touch you the way you want to be touched. Cass, let me love you … like you need to be loved."

"I can't," she sobbed. "I can't let you hurt anymore. All I bring you … is … is pain, Julian!"

Julian spun her around to face him in the darkness and he dried her cheeks. "You don't bring me pain, Cass. You release me from it. Release me from it now."

His mouth covered hers and he kissed her long and hard. She gasped for a breath when his fingers unbuttoned her dress, and he reached inside to caress her breasts. His lips tingled her neck at all the tender points. Julian knew her. He knew her better than she knew herself.

It frightened her when he slowly lifted the flowing cotton material of her dress. It sent electric sensations up her thighs in anticipation like fire to paper. He lifted her body then; easing into her as she wrapped her legs around his narrow hips, and waves of pleasure sent tiny shocks to her intoxicated brain. Her long nails clawed his bare back and she could feel his muscles twitch from the excitement of the pain. All at once they were on the floor and she arched to meet each thrust of his desperate need to make her come with him. When she did, her body shuddered and shook beneath him and she moved to kiss his lips and lay and embraced for a long time before he picked her up.

"Talk to me," he breathed as he paced the floor with her.

"It's better that you don't know."

"If he hurts you again, I'll kill him, Cass. I swear it," he finished.

"I know," she replied. "I know."

For hours he paced, rocking her from side to side, whispering his words of love to her. Cassidy lay next to him gently caressing his chest until he fell asleep. It was hard for her to leave the warmth of his body, but she knew already that Roman would be furious when she came in so late.

CHAPTER FIFTEEN

After parking in the garage she sat to smoke one last cigarette before the door was thrown open and she was thrown up against it before Roman slammed it shut. "Where have you been?"

"I went for a drive," she replied.

"Went for a drive, where?"

"I was at the bar," Cassidy stated.

"You are a liar!" he shouted, as he slapped her across the face.

Cassidy felt the sting of his hand when she lifted her fingers to her lip, she realized she was bleeding. She smiled with tears rolling down her face. "I don't care anymore, Roman. You do what you feel you have to, and when you're finished, I won't have to feel anything anymore. Then you won't have to love me, and I won't have to hate you."

"Shut up! You make me sick!"

"No," she said. "You make me sick. You can do whatever you want and I can't? Do you really think you can continue beating the hell out of me and get away with it? How much longer do you think it will be before my brother comes after you?"

"I said shut up," he replied.

Roman gathered her up and shoved her inside the house. She stumbled into the kitchen and braced herself with the countertop. When she looked over at the clock it read 4:30 a.m. Cassidy almost had to laugh at her stupidity in coming home at all. She should have stayed wrapped warmly in Julian's body. She should have walked to Mason's and passed out on the staircase.

Her husband forced her to turn around and face him. He was irate and seething and she still couldn't comprehend why she'd come home. It struck her when his fist hit her in the stomach and she fell to the hard cool floor trying to catch her breath. He stood there watching her without sympathy.

"You won't make a fool out of me any longer," he said, as he snatched a handful of hair and started dragging her up the stairs. "He's a dead man, Cassidy. Maybe not today or tomorrow but, I'll be waiting for the right moment."

"Roman, wait!" she screamed. "Oh God, please stop!"

He paused and turned to release her. She used him to pull herself up as she fought the pain in her middle. She gathered his shirt collar into her hands and smiled. Roman just stared at her strangely.

"Now, you take me to the hospital you miserable, bastard. You just killed your unborn baby!"

He pushed her away and she fell back to her knees and folded forward as she cried. Roman just stood there in shock watching her. Blood was now in a pool and smearing across the rug as she was crawling to the nearest phone. The pain was overwhelming her and she couldn't even see where she was going. Then suddenly Cassidy couldn't feel anything and the room seemed to spin and become hazy.

She knocked the phone off the table but couldn't hear

anything but the deafening stale tone. Everything went blank as she passed out, and Roman picked her up and carried her to his car. He trembled with fear as his hands gripped the steering wheel and noticed that they were covered in his wife's blood. In his panic he couldn't think, and drove to the gate of his brother-in-law's estate. He paused only to lean over and open the door long enough to shove Cassidy out on the pavement. He screeched off as the security guard made a call for an ambulance and then to the house before he rushed out to gather Cassidy's limp body into his arms.

Mason charged out of his home and down the driveway barefoot, wearing a pair of jeans. Julian was startled awake by the sounds of the siren of the ambulance and shouting voices. He walked out on his balcony to see the blinding red lights and Mason holding his sister, as his voice cracked and faltered, as he answered the paramedics questions. Julian threw on his robe on rushed out as they were bringing out the gurney. Lacey moved to see him coming and jumped up to try and hold him back with tears running down her cheeks.

"Julian, don't! You don't want to see her now," she exclaimed.

"Let me go!" he snapped and moved passed her.

Lacey put her face in her hands. Mason was holding his sister's loose hand as the paramedics carefully lifted her onto the gurney. She was wearing an oxygen mask.

"Cass? Oh God," Julian said, kneeling to take her other hand. "What happened?"

"Sir, we have to take her now," one paramedic exclaimed.

"Let me go with her," Julian said, as he smoothed back her tangled hair.

"Go and get dressed, Jule. I'll go," Mason replied in a gentle voice.

"I have to be with her," Julian insisted.

"Only family can go with her now. Now get dressed and I'll see you there. All right?" He knew he couldn't keep Julian away.

"OK," Julian nodded, and watched his friend climb into the back of the ambulance. He felt Lacey touch his shoulder and he turned to her and she fell into his arms. "Where's Julianna?"

"She's asleep in the house," she replied.

"I'll call you as soon as I know something," he finished then ran in to get dressed.

Mason met Julian as he strode down the hallway. He gave Mason a change of clothes and waited for him to change impatiently. "They're with her now. I don't know what is going on, yet."

"I want to be with her. I can't take this anymore," Julian strained. "You want to make this easy on me Mason, tell me what happened."

"All I know is Roman pulled up to the gate and pushed her out before he drove away," Mason shrugged.

"Why didn't she stay with me last night?" he mumbled, numbed with his fear of losing her.

"What?"

"She was with me last night. We talked. She was very drunk. I knew something was bothering her, but she said it was better that I didn't know," Julian explained.

"Because she's pregnant, Jule. The bastard ..." Mason

faltered, and had to clear his throat to continue. "The bastard raped her. I tried to get her to come with us after the birthday party, but she just ran off. Lacey said the gynecologist called. Cassie didn't know for sure until they called. She was really upset. It must have been late when she came over."

"After the bar closed. I asked her to stay. I should have made her stay."

"Julian, it's not your fault." Mason put his had on his friend's shoulder.

"It is my fault! If I wouldn't have been such a fool, I'd have married her no matter what, and given her the life Lacey has. A happy one."

"No," Mason shook his head. "That's my fault."

"I'm going to wait until I know she's all right. Then I'm going after the son of a bitch. When I get my hands on him this time, I won't let go," Julian swore.

"You can't touch him, Jule. Cassidy can't press charges if you maim him. I was going to find him, too, but the police can't even find him. He must have dragged her all over the house. They said there's blood everywhere."

It was hours before the doctor came out. He looked tired, but smiled slightly and knelt to where Julian and Mason were sitting. He explained that she had a miscarriage, and she'd been bruised and cut from being knocked around. Then he said he wanted to keep her for a few days so she could get some rest and her strength back. Mason stood and patted his friend on the back.

"You go on in first. I'm going to call Lacey," Mason smiled with relief.

"Thanks, Mason," Julian said.

He nodded and walked to the payphone. Julian pushed open the door to Cassidy's room. She was awake staring at the walls blankly. He closed his eyes and took a deep breath before exhaling, and smiled. She didn't even realize he was there until she felt him take her hand. Then she looked over at him slowly.

"How are you, sweetheart?" he asked.

"Julian," she breathed and tried to move, but couldn't.

"Hey. Rest now, I'm here." He kissed her fingers. "Look what he's done to you. Leave him. I'm begging you to leave him. You and Julianna can live with me. Promise me."

"You — have to go ... away," she croaked. "Do this for ... me, Jule. Go far away."

"Only if you'll come with me," he stated.

"I can't. He'll never ... let ... go," Cassidy strained as he dried tears that rolled across her temples.

Julian ran his hand through her hair and smiled, not knowing how to feel. "Good God, Cass. You're not going back to him are you? Not after last night."

"I'm trying to ... protect you," she cried.

"I can take care of myself. Don't worry about me. All I care about is you. Cassidy, I love you."

Cassidy was silent as she squeezed her eyes and then gathered what was left of her strength to push him away. "Did you hear what I said, Drake? Go ... away! I don't want to see you anymore! Get ... out! Get out!"

"Cassidy, don't be like this. Please."

"I ... want you out." She coughed and fell back weakly. "Get out."

Julian stood. "All right. I'll go but don't you come back

to me, Cassidy Spencer. Don't you come back to me in the middle of the night, and tell me you love me. If you did love me, you'd leave him before he kills you." He left as his eyes burned with tears.

Julian tore out of the hospital parking lot. Tears swelled in his eyes and rolled down his cheeks. He wanted to be the white knight who rode in on his noble steed. He wanted to lift Cassidy in his arms and ride away with her. His eyes were so flooded he had to pull off the road or collide with opposing traffic. He sat in the car and beat his fists on the steering wheel, before he gripped it tightly.

Lacey cradled the phone when Julian stormed into Mason's den. She watched him as he poured himself a glass of scotch and swallowed it in one gulp. When he seemed to calm, he focused on Mason's gun collection. Julian walked to the cabinet in long steps, and braced himself as he scanned the many polished rifles.

"Julian, what are you doing?" Lacey asked carefully.

"Give me the keys to this cabinet, Lacey."

"Not a chance. Let's have another drink. Even I can use one today," she retorted.

Julian moved to shatter the glass and Lacey gasped before he caught himself and strode out of the room and went back out to his car. He drove around the spraying fountain and slammed his car in park. Lacey came outside to see him shoving shells into his own rifle before getting back in his car, and screeching out onto the road.

There was still a police car in Cassidy's driveway when Julian pulled onto her street. He took a deep breath and let it out trying to calm himself, as he sat at the corner. Then after a few minutes decided that the situation was out of his hands. When he came through the gate, the guard phoned Lacey that he had returned. Lacey thanked him and went to check on Julian.

Julian was pacing his den back and forth.

"Julian, are you all right?"

"No," he smiled and shook his head. "I'm hurt and angry, but I've calmed down."

"Thank God," Lacey breathed.

"She's afraid for me. She wants me to go away. Why, Lacey? Why?" His voice caught in his throat.

"Because she loves you, Jule," Lacey replied and embraced him.

CHAPTER SIXTEEN

"Cassie, what are you doing? Are you out of your mind?" Mason asked. He couldn't believe his ears.

"Maybe," she replied, and he looked away.

They were sitting in his office with a police officer. She wouldn't press any charges against Roman and decided to bail him out of jail. The officer shook his head and stood before he shook Mason's hand and he left. Cassidy was sitting turning the ring on her finger over and over again. Mason slammed his hand down on his desk and then turned away to stare out the window.

"Before I go, Mason, I want to give you and Lacey temporary custody of Julianna. Can I count on you to do this for me?"

"I'm warning you right now that if you do this I will take her away completely," he threatened.

"Then, I'll fight you on it," she snapped.

"Then I guarantee we'll both go bankrupt in court costs and attorney fees."

"Touché," she smiled. "Mason, I love you. I know you don't understand, and I'm not even sure I do, but I need you. I need you to do this for me. It's not like I'll be a stranger. It's not like I'm abandoning her."

"No. It's because you're afraid of what he might do to her," he said matter-of-factly.

"You're right," she admitted. "I am."

"Stop this. What are you trying to prove? Or are you just going to commit suicide?" Mason asked as he leaned over his desk.

Cassidy sighed and stood up. "I'm doing this for Julian, Mason. I want you to send him away. Make something up. I don't care. Give him something to do in the States. And, don't tell him anything except you can't go."

"Now, you want me to send him away. I've just spent two years apologizing and, you're right. I don't understand."

"I don't want him to get hurt, OK?" She started to cry. "I'm scared that Roman will try to hurt him. And, that's all I'm gonna to say."

Mason sat hard in his chair after she grabbed her purse and left slamming the door behind her. He wanted to run after her and shake some real sense into her, but knew she had to be alone. She wasn't thinking clearly. But, he prayed that she would start.

Cassidy bailed her husband out of jail after he agreed to sign the documents giving Mason and Lacey temporary custody of their daughter.

As their life continued, he seemed to stay away from her more and more every day. Of course, he was hardly at the gallery that she was completely running on her own, and only came home when he wanted a change of clothes and some money.

Julian caught on to his friend's false job in New York and smiled as he tossed the paperwork back on his desk and walked out of the room. He wasn't fooled with Mason's attempt to please his sister, but at least he could say Mason tried.

Julian started drinking heavily after that. He stayed locked up in his den or office, and spent his nights down at his favorite bar. He wasn't taking Cassidy's denying him very well. Julian loved Cassidy and nothing was going to take it away from him as far as he was concerned. One night, he sat in front of her house all day waiting for Roman to leave.

When he did and he was sure he was out of sight, Julian got out of his car in the pouring rain. He let the thunder roll and the lightening flash as he was baptized in the cool rain. Then he went up to the door and rang the doorbell. Cassidy hurried down the stairs in her nightgown wondering who would be coming over so late in the rotten weather. She paused when she saw him soaking and dripping in the doorway.

"Go away," she said, and moved to close the door.

"No," he replied, pulling her against him into the rain. "You still love me."

"It doesn't matter," Cassidy replied not really trying to push him away, but making an effort to look like she wanted to.

He held her tight and pressed his lips to hers as he brought his fingers up through her wet hair. Now they were both soaked and laying half in and half out of the doorway. When he pulled away and started to get up, Cassidy tugged him back to her and covered his mouth with hers again to taste the fine whiskey he had been drinking. Hoping maybe to join him in intoxication to feel what he was feeling. When he looked back into her eyes, they were content from making love with wild abandon. Julian touched her face once more and helped her up.

Cassidy threw her arms around his neck. "Sometimes there's a way, Cass. I love you like there's no tomorrow."

She wanted to speak but he hushed her with his forefinger and backed away before he turned and jogged down the driveway. Cassidy felt her body shivering as she stood in the doorway. He disappeared into the storm just as he'd come. It was strange when Roman came home and automatically picked her up and put her in bed, trying to take away her chill. Then he carefully left her alone in the guestroom to sleep.

Lacey carried a tray of dinner over to Julian. She took his empty rum bottle and tossed it in the trash. Then she dumped the overflowing ashtrays and sat down in front of him to open the tray. Julian turned up his nose and tried to get her to put it away. She laughed at him when he reached for the bottle that wasn't there anymore.

"Stop it. How can you sit there and laugh at a drunken man?" he asked.

"Julian, you need a little humor in your life. You're incredibly too serious all the time now. I'm trying to help you. Please eat a little," she said.

"Is that why you came over here?"

"Why do you sit here pathetically in a liquor bottle? It's not going to solve anything. Why do you keep it up?"

"If I drink enough sometimes I can get my mind off of Cassidy," he revealed.

"Get over her. It's ruining your life. She's forbidden and you have to move on. Find someone else," Lacey suggested.

"Like who, Rachelle? Maybe I should start seeing Shalane Taylor? What a joke," he replied with sarcasm.

"Mason was sent a telegram not too long ago from Shalane. She has scammed some wealthy man into marrying her. He told me all about her. He really appreciated what you did for him," she explained.

"Yeah? He had a funny way of showing his gratitude," Julian sighed. "Lacey, I can't talk to you now. I'll only end up saying something to hurt you or Mason. It's better if you leave me alone for now."

"All right. At least try to eat something, Julian." She stood.

"I'll try." He half smiled thanking her the best he could.

Lacey came in and hung up her coat and went to sit with her husband in front of the television. Julian's skin was pale and he'd grown thin from not eating. He only sat there night after night staring into the fire. Mason put his arm around his wife knowing that she was worried about his friend.

"Mason, I'm afraid Julian might do something to hurt himself. You're his best friend, yet you let him sit and drink himself away. Why can't you understand?"

"I told him I understood. I told him, my sister and him have my blessing, but I can't give him what he wants. It's out of my hands," Mason admitted.

CHAPTER SEVENTEEN

Mason watched Cassidy and Julianna sitting on a blanket playing with a bucket of blocks in the studio. Mason never mentioned that she looked good, but still deeply sad when he caught her eyes for longer than a minute. Julianna clapped and they sang as she tried in babyish tongue. Cassidy laughed and looked up to see Julian come out of his office to hand something to Mason. She hadn't even known he was there.

She stood quickly to view a man she'd never seen before. Julian's beautiful eyes were glassed over. His hair was uncombed and there was no color left in his complexion. Mason watched his sister's expression go from amused to heartbroken. Julian offered her a shattered form of a smile and went back into his office.

"Dear God, Mason, what's happening to him?" she choked.

"I never wanted you to see him this way. I thought he'd snap out of it, but his drinking gets worse every day. He needs you, Cassie. I'll use all my power to get you that divorce. Lacey worries about him so much she checks on him constantly at night; afraid he'll kill himself with alcohol poisoning. Go to him."

"Roman — " she was cut off.

"Roman can go to hell for all I care. The only people I care about are you and Julian right now," Mason stressed, slamming his hand down on his desk.

All the shades were pulled down in Julian's office. Empty bottles of liquor lay on the bar. Several ashtrays were so filled that they were overflowing. The air was thick and sour smelling of smoke, booze, and a little of cologne. Julian sat with his face in his hands. Cassidy knelt next to him and slowly stroked his hair. He looked at her with tears in his eyes.

"Leave me alone. I don't want you to see me like this. Go now. I don't want to hurt you," he said sternly.

"No. I won't go. I won't let you do this to yourself anymore. I want to help you," she replied defiantly.

"Help me. Why? So you can make it all better and go back to the bastard and let him run your life?" he questioned with amusement. "I can't let you do that to me again, Cassidy. Get out! I can't stand the sight of you!" Julian shouted and pushed her away.

"I'm not leaving you. Not this time."

He poured himself another drink. Cassidy snatched the glass and bottle from him and threw them to shatter against the wall. Then she went to the bar and starting smashing all the full bottles of booze she could find. Julian grabbed her angrily and pushed her to the floor. Cassidy got back up and slapped him across the face as hard as she could.

"I won't let you do it! I won't let you drink your life away! You can beat the hell out of me, and I'll get back up and fight for you. I need you, Julian Drake, and you're no good to me six feet under. Please, Jule, please," she begged him. "Let me back in. I promise you that I won't let you down this time."

Julian sank to the floor on his knees and looked up at her. Cassidy knelt with him and he hugged her tightly. She held him tight against her, and then they kissed passionately, long and hard. When he pulled away, he smiled at her with hope in his eyes. Suddenly he fell against her and she felt a sharp pain in her shoulder.

Cassidy looked up in the doorway to see Roman standing there. Smoke floated from the end of the gun he held. It dropped to the floor from his fingers, as Cassidy pulled Julian upright. Warm blood covered her hands when she looked down at them. Roman knelt by her in shock and was trying to apologize. Cassidy heard someone screaming, but didn't realize that it was herself. Julian put his hand on her face and, she held it there with her own as tears mixed with blood.

"I will always love you, Cass. Nothing can take that away from me, not even death," Julian gasped for breath.

"You aren't going to die. You'll be all right. You'll see. Hold on, please!" Cassidy begged.

Mason rushed into the room. He had only been in the bathroom for a minute changing Julianna when he heard the shot. He called the police and an ambulance and threw himself to the floor with his sister and his friend. Julianna was screaming from her playpen. Cassidy was so hysterical that she didn't even realize that the strength of the bullet had passed through Julian and was lodged in her shoulder.

"Kiss me, Cassidy. Kiss me and call me Jule one last time. Tell me that you love me."

"Jule, an ambulance is on the way. Hold on friend," Mason said.

"Jule, please don't let go. I love you so much."

"I want you to breathe my last breath, Cass. Kiss me."

Tears fell from her eyes onto his cheeks as she covered his mouth with her own and kissed him so painfully it brought tears to Mason's eyes. Julian used all of his remaining strength to return her kiss. He fell back and his breath escaped him and his body was lifeless. Cassidy looked up at her brother, heartbroken. She pulled Julian against her and rocked him back and forth.

"No, no, no. Please, oh God, no. You can't take him away from me now!" Cassidy cried as she shook him trying to wake him up in terror.

Paramedics rushed in and pulled him away from her. Two policemen came in and handcuffed Roman while reading his rights. Cassidy stood up as another paramedic helped her. She pushed him away and picked up the pistol from the floor and pointed it at her husband. Everyone paused and quietly tried to talk her out of it. She was angry and crazy with grief, and all she could see was him beating her again and again with no remorse even when she crawled bleeding to the telephone.

"It's not worth it, Cassie. Don't do it," Mason said gently.

"All I have to do is pull the trigger," she sniffed. "It's just you and me now, Roman. How does it feel to be at the other end?"

"If you do it now, Cassidy, whose going to explain to Julianna why you're in prison and why she can't see you?" Mason pointed out when they heard the child cry out.

When her face crumpled, Cassidy handed her brother the pistol and he gave it to the officer, as he tugged his sister into his arms. On a stretcher they put Julian and covered his face with a sheet. Cassidy turned when she saw his arm drop from the side and something fell from his hand. Mason bent down to pick up the gold band. Cassidy smiled through her tears as she slipped it on her finger next to the diamond and sapphire one she'd worn for years. When Mason looked closely, the band he picked up matched the one she was wearing.

Roman's trial didn't last long. He was sentenced to prison for the rest of his life. When he stood up and they handcuffed him, Cassidy stood up with her brother and sister-in-law, and Julianna. That's when he noticed Cassidy's belly was swollen with Julian's child. She smiled at him and paused in front of him so he could kiss his daughter good-bye.

"It's a boy, Roman. Julian might be gone, but his son will be his namesake." She smiled and walked away before they took him in the opposite direction.

***

Printed in the United States
971200002B